THE IRREPROACHABLE RIVAL

Cautiously Calista asked Mr. Witton about his fiancee. "Is she . . . is she conventional?"

"Extremely," Witton said. "She would not think of going out without her maid or a groom. She is an expert needlewoman, excels in the use of watercolors, sings like an angel, and plays the pianoforte effortlessly."

There was a pause. "She sounds quite perfect," Calista said at last, reflecting on her own lack of these accomplishments. "I am surprised you can bear to be away from her side."

"Oh," Witton said airily, "she will be waiting for me whenever I can see her again."

"Indeed?" Calista said, gripping the edge of her work table tightly. "Does she love you so very much? Do you love her?"

Then she braced herself for the answer sure to come from this gentleman who was as impossible for her to win as he was to resist. . . .

APRIL KIHLSTROM was born in Buffalo, New York, and graduated from Cornell University with an M.S. in Operations Research. She lives with her husband and their two children in New Jersey.

SIGNET REGENCY ROMANCE

COMING IN MARCH 1989

Ellen Fitzgerald
An Unwelcome Alliance

Carla Kelly
Summer Campaign

Emily Hendrickson
Hidden Inheritance

THE SCHOLAR'S DAUGHTER
APRIL KIHLSTROM

A SIGNET BOOK

NEW AMERICAN LIBRARY

Copyright©1989 by April Kihlstrom

SIGNET TRADEMARK REG.U.S.PAT. OFF. AND FOREIGN COUNTRIES
REGISTERED TRADEMARK—MARCA REGISTRADA
HECHO EN CHICAGO, U.S.A.

SIGNET, SIGNET CLASSIC, MENTOR, ONYX, PLUME,
MERIDIAN and NAL BOOKS are published by
NAL PENGUIN INC., 1633 Broadway,
New York, New York 10019

First Printing, February 1989

1 2 3 4 5 6 7 8 9

PRINTED IN THE UNITED STATES OF AMERICA

$\mathbf{F}$REDERICK LEVERTON STOOD by the fireplace in his library holding a glass of excellent brandy in one hand and looking down at his well-shod foot. Nearby, his wife, Eleanor, dressed in a becoming gown of pale green satin with embroidered lace at the hem, watched him with a warmth undimmed by the past two years of marriage. His closest friend, John Witton, was ensconced in the most comfortable chair in the room, neatly dressed in fawn pantaloons and a brown coat that fitted his shoulders closely. If there were a fault to be found with Witton's appearance, it was that his shirt points were of a more moderate height and his cravat more simply tied than Leverton's.

"Are you quite certain there is no mistake, Freddy?" Witton was asking with a frown. "It seems extraordinary that you should be named guardian to a pack of brats you have not seen and whose father was not a particular friend of your family."

Leverton smiled good-naturedly at his friend. "Ah, but there was a method to Oliver Standish's madness," he said solemnly. "Standish contemplated, I believe, a marriage between his second daughter, Calista, and myself."

That produced a most satisfying effect. "But you are already married," Witton protested, setting his glass down with a snap.

Leverton hesitated a moment, then said, a smile beginning to form about his mouth, "Well, to be fair, John, the will only stated that Miss Standish must marry before her twenty-first birthday if she wished to inherit a substantial amount of money. As she is, I collect, already twenty years of age, that does not give her a great deal of time. That would be her affair, of course, save that the solicitor had a letter for me in which Oliver Standish hinted that he thought I might make a match of it with the girl. I assure you there was no mistaking the meaning of his words."

"Was the man mad? What did he expect you to do?" Witton demanded.

"Poison me," Eleanor suggested promptly, with a mischievous gleam in her eye.

Leverton directed an affectionate smile at his wife as he eplied, "Stuff and nonsense, you pea-goose! You know Standish wrote his will before we were married."

"But that was over two years ago," Witton pointed out impatiently.

"Precisely," Eleanor said with relish. "That is why I think it must be poison or some such thing that he had in mind."

With a snort of disgust, or perhaps it was a sigh

of resignation, Leverton said, "Anyone who has ever known Standish would realize that he might never have been aware that I was married. The man was a scholar with, according to my uncle, Sir Charles, a brilliant mind for academics and not the slightest day-to-day sense whatsoever. Standish is the funny fellow I told you about, John, that time I went to Oxford to see my uncle. Standish happened to be there and we got into a discussion about Socrates, remember? Well, anyway, Standish must have taken a fancy to me, written his will and the letter, and then I suppose forgotten the matter. Or if he did recall and did know that I had married, never got around to altering the will. Or destroying the letter. I shudder to think what state his affairs are in now."

"But you need not deal with those, surely," Witton protested.

Leverton smiled his easy smile again. "No, no, there are solicitors for most of that. But I am particularly requested to call upon the bereaved family and see that everything is in order on their home estate near Chippenham."

"And I," Eleanor said with a mock pout, "am not allowed to go with him."

A twinkle appeared in Witton's usually grave eyes as he replied, "Indeed, I should think not! What if the daughter should take after her father? You would bo so conveniently at hand to poison."

Leverton, who had moved to stand behind his

wife's chair, now placed a hand on each shoulder and said quietly, "I know it is very hard, my love, to be so hemmed about, but the doctor and I will not have you risk traveling so soon after the birth of the baby."

Holding tight to one of the hands on her shoulder, Eleanor said, a trifle anxiously, "I know you will not be gone long, but I confess I shall miss you sadly."

"Can you not delay a while," Witton asked with another frown, "until Eleanor's health will permit her to accompany you?"

"That will not be for some time yet, John. The birth was very difficult for Eleanor and I do not wish to run any risks with her now," Leverton replied with a sigh. "And quite frankly, I should like to have the business over and done with."

From his chair Witton cleared his throat and said, "Shall I come with you, Freddy? That way," he told Eleanor with a gleam in his own eye, "I can keep him out of mischief!"

"*I* should like that above all things," Eleanor said immediately. "Of course, I should like it better if you could go in his stead, but as you cannot, this must do."

"Do? Of course it shall do," Freddy retorted lightly as he came around his wife's chair to sit between Eleanor and Witton. "It will be another adventure for John and myself to share. Indeed, my love, it may answer perfectly. I shall marry John to Calista and then everyone, including Oliver Standish, will be satisfied."

Eleanor laughed and Witton permitted himself a thin smile. "I see what it is. You mean to make me the target of a matchmaking family. In that case, I thank you, no. I would far rather stay in London," Witton said coolly.

"Where, of course, such a thing could never happen to you," Leverton said cordially.

In spite of himself, Witton laughed and Leverton went on, "Eleanor is only roasting you. Even if the Standishes did try to matchmake, I can scarcely imagine anyone making you do something against your will." Witton merely regarded his friend with patent disbelief and Leverton went on, coaxingly, "You do mean to come with me, John, don't you? You've nothing else here that requires your attention and you have just been telling us how bored you are with the London Season. Come with me, instead, and keep me company." He paused, then added superbly, "Unless, of course, you mean to post down to Witton Manor?"

At that Witton gave a start. Grimly he replied, "No, I have no intention of doing so, I can assure you."

"How is Edwin? And your mother?" Eleanor asked.

Witton shrugged. "My mother is as usual. I confess to some slight concern about Edwin. Certainly it is time he paid a visit to London, though as you can well imagine, my mother is against the scheme."

"She has kept him remarkably close to home," Leverton said with a frown. "Particularly for as high-spirited a boy as I recall him to be."

"You need only add that as his guardian it is my duty to counter such mollycoddling and you will have said everything I have said to myself," Witton retorted a trifle bitterly. "Understand, however, that it is not entirely my fault. He has shown no desire to visit me here and, indeed, refused when I wrote to suggest it."

"What?" Leverton demanded, thunderstruck. "I should have thought he would be delighted to escape from his mother's skirts."

"So should I," Witton said grimly.

"There must be a girl in it," Eleanor pronounced wisely, leaning forward in her chair.

"I agree," Witton replied. "And if he does not accept my next invitation I suppose I shall have to post down to Witton Manor after all and see for myself. After we visit the Standish family, perhaps." He paused, then added severely, addressing Eleanor, "Though mind, it's not to marry any heiresses, only to keep Freddy out of mischief that I am going."

"Nonsense!" Freddy retorted lightly as he rose out of his chair. "You are no more sensible than I am. Everyone just assumes you are because you wear that Friday face and refuse to employ the services of a really top-flight valet."

"Well, I shall be very disappointed if nothing comes of it," Eleanor said with a distinct sniff. A moment later, however, her eyes were twinkling as she added, "But only if it is what you wish,

John. I want to see you happy. After all, Freddy and I owe our happiness in part to your help three years ago."

"I confess" Witton said gravely, "that when I see you and Freddy together it is almost possible to believe that one could enjoy being tenant-for-life with someone."

"There, you see?" Leverton said with a grin. "I told you it would answer perfectly."

"I said," Witton replied dryly, "that it was *almost* possible. I've yet to meet the female who would suit me as well as Eleanor suits you."

Freddy turned serious as he said, "All joking aside, John, it is my fervent hope that one day you shall do so. As for Miss Standish, you need not regard any of what I have said. If you like, we can even pretend your affections are already attached. Though I've no doubt Miss Standish's family would be appalled to learn of the letter her father wrote me and of his intentions. I just want company on this tedious chore of a visit. And you are the fellow whose company I most enjoy, God knows why!"

And upon that amiable note, they turned their attention to the brandy and whether or not it was superior to that laid down by Witton's grandfather.

In the drawing room of the Standish household, a far more disordered room than Leverton's library, Mrs. Standish had just finished giving directions to the housekeeper for the next day's activities. When the woman had gone from the room, Amabel Standish was left alone with her daughter, Calista. Even a stranger, seeing them together, must have known they were related. To be sure, Mrs. Standish had fair hair pulled neatly back from her face under her lace cap and Calista's brown hair showed a distinct disposition to curl, but they were both petite women with the same delicate features and an intelligent air about them. And both, at the moment, were dressed in black dresses of merino wool, a color far more becoming to the mother than the daughter.

It was fortunate that both women were ignorant of the letter Mr. Leverton had received from the solicitor. Otherwise they would have felt even more consternation than they already did at the notion of his arrival.

As it was, Mrs. Standish said, "I am a trifle worried, Calista. Mr. Leverton must be expected to come to visit us, as your father's will requested, and we must provide for his comfort as well as for his wife's, but I haven't the least notion what they are like."

Quietly Calista rose to her feet and took a turn about the room before she spoke. It was not her custom to act impulsively and in that she differed greatly from her father. With quiet deliberation she asked, "Why did Papa name Mr. Leverton as guardian to us, Mama? Papa scarcely knew the man and we don't know him at all."

Mrs. Standish's reply was an echo of Leverton's. "I have no doubt," she said, "that he took a fancy to the poor man. If he were not already married, I would suspect that your father thought it a good way to throw the man into your company. After all, your father did seem preoccupied with the notion of your marriage."

"Preoccupied?" Calista echoed in calm disbelief. "Only after his death, you mean. When he was alive he made every effort to discourage the few young men who came to call upon me. And now, in his will he states that I must marry before my twenty-first birthday or the ten thousand pounds I will otherwise inherit goes straight to his old university!"

Mrs. Standish's eyes reflected her daughter's unhappiness. "I know, Calista, that it must seem most unfair. Indeed, I cannot think what your father was about or why he did not consult me upon the matter. The solicitor said he was entirely unable to deflect your father from his determined course. In fairness, I must say, however, that your father did write the will some years ago and could not have known how little time he would be allowing you to find a husband."

"What would he have done if I were already twenty-one and not married?" Calista demanded. "The condition would have been impossible to fulfill."

Mrs. Standish sighed. "The solicitor said that he asked your father that very question and was told that before then the age would have been changed to twenty-five. I must confess that I wish he had already done so. There are less than twelve months to your twenty-first birthday and how could he expect you to meet anyone while you were in mourning?"

"Papa would no doubt say that if I only showed sufficient resolution the matter could be resolved in a trice. After all, if he did not regard convention, why should I? That is what he would say if he were here. Oh, Mama, I wish he had never made such a provision at all," Calista said bitterly.

"It was meant out of love," Mrs. Standish tried to explain. "You know that in the will your father said that Amethyst was already provided for and that Xanthe—"

Abruptly, Mrs. Standish broke off as she recollected what her husband had said about Xanthe. Quietly, Calista finished the sentence for her. " . . . and that Xanthe was so pretty he need not worry about her, but that I showed no inclination to marry and he meant to give me a reason to do so. Oh, yes, Mama, I remember very well what Papa wrote in his will. And I can guess that, selfish as he was in life, he did not wish to lose my abilities as an assistant. But after death, oh, why then, he is amiable enough to wish to see me wed."

"Calista!" her mother remonstrated. "You must not speak of your father that way. He is dead!"

"And must that blind me to his faults?" Calista asked evenly. "I cannot see that death has altered them in any way." She paused, then added, the constraint evident in her voice, "I can only wonder what Mr. Leverton makes of all this."

With dignity, Mrs. Standish replied, "Our solicitor said that Mr. Leverton was quite understanding, quite the gentleman about the whole thing. Which shows that your father was not entirely lacking in taste."

"Just lacking in discretion and common sense and concern for my feelings," Calista concluded dryly. "Why didn't Papa consult with me if he was so concerned about my marriage?"

"Yes, well, he ought to have consulted both of us. But he did not, and what's done is done and we must make the best of it," her mother said with a sigh. "Meanwhile, Mr. Leverton's visit must be our immediate concern. I am hoping he will make a token visit to the estate, we shall entertain him for a day or so, we shall thank him for his kindness, and then he will leave and that will be that. His guardianship duties are of the lightest, you know. He is only to give me advice, he has no real power to order any of you about. The only difficulty is in how to entertain him when he comes."

"P'rhaps we shouldn't and then he will leave all the sooner," Calista suggested impishly.

"Calista!" Mrs. Standish said in outrage. "One cannot treat a guest that way! We must make some effort. And suppose Mrs. Leverton accompanies him? One cannot wish to slight her! Though I confess I don't think that likely unless they are on their way somewhere else and we are along their route. The rains have left the roads in a horrible state this spring."

Calista, who had learned some time since that life with Mr. Standish had robbed her mother of whatever sense of humor she had once possessed, sighed and changed the subject. "When does Amethyst return home?" she asked.

"At no time soon, I fear. She says that she is still feeling unwell," Mrs. Standish said quietly. "And that is another thing I cannot like. I think Amethyst is merely pampering herself and making altogether too much of this business of having a baby. Meanwhile, Mr. Trumble must wish to return to his own home. He has said so more than once to me."

"And yet," Calista replied dryly, "he has shown no signs of impatience to the rest of us. Indeed, he appears quite content to roam about the country-side on horse or foot discovering all of our local pubs."

"Calista!" her mother remonstrated, again appalled. "Really, you must learn to curb your hoydenish tongue. Whatever will Mr. Leverton think of you?"

"As Mr. Leverton is already married," Calista said wth a shrug, "I cannot see that it signifies."

With a look of horror, Mrs. Standish threw up her hands in disgust. "Whatever am I to do with you?" she asked. "Your father has irrevocably spoiled you. You are not only a bluestocking, but he has taught you the most horrid ideas and manners of speech."

Again Calista sighed. More, she rose and walked over to the window where she sat on the cushioned seat there and tried to cope with the fresh waves of grief breaking over her. After a moment she said, the constraint again evident in her voice, "You have said that Papa detested roundaboutation. Well, and so do I. If that must make me a bluestocking and hoydenish, then so be it. I will not give up the known pleasures of the mind that Papa showed me for the dubious pleasures of proper femininity."

"And just who am I going to marry you off to, then?" Mrs. Standish asked her daughter tartly. "For marry I am determined you shall." A stormy expression appeared on Calista's face and Mrs. Standish added hastily, "Even if we don't care about your father's will, there are other reasons to see you married. Gilby will be of age in three years and perhaps looking about him for a wife. Once he is wed it shall be the dower house for me and I cannot believe you will be comfortable there."

"Aunt Hester left me a comfortable portion, perhaps I shall travel," Calista replied bravely.

"Oh, Calista, it is the merest competence!" Mrs. Standish cried, her face expressing her distress. "And you cannot mean to become an eccentric? Whatever will people say?"

"Whatever they wish, I expect," Calista said with a tolerable appearance of tranquility.

Mrs. Standish knew well enough the stubborn look on her second daughter's face. In a softer tone she said, "There is no reasoning with you now. It is still too soon after your father's death and you cannot help but feel this way."

I shall always feel this way, Calista thought mutinously, but she did not say so aloud. Mrs. Standish unbent so far as to go over to her daughter as she sat in the window seat and rest a hand reassuringly on her shoulder. Calista smiled gratefully and then Mrs. Standish turned and left the room to check on her eldest daughter, Amethyst.

2

OLIVER AND AMABEL Standish had had five children. Amethyst was the eldest and had, at twenty-three, been married for some time to George Trumble. The other children, in order of age, were Calista, Gilby, Raynor, and Xanthe. Visitors were inclined to find them a merry bunch and so they generally were when they were not quarreling as siblings so often do.

This particular morning, to the despair of Mrs. Standish, they were quarreling and in the most ridiculous way. It had begun with the two boys, Gilby and Raynor, roasting their elder sister, Calista.

"I think Cal should poison Mrs. Leverton," Gilby said impishly. "Then she can marry him and fulfull the terms of Papa's will, as a good girl would. After all, who else is there at hand? She hasn't much time, you know."

Calista, who was busy with her needle mending her brothers' shirts, was not amused. Another time she might have been, but today she had been dreaming daydreams of her own, of a prince, or at any rate a gentleman, who might come along some day and rescue her from—from what? She could not say. But the daydreams left her restless and anxious, and she snapped at Gilby's teasing. "Don't be absurd," she said sharply.

"Yes, don't be," Raynor added with apparent sympathy. "I should know she had done it and be obliged to tell the authorities. And that wouldn't do at all."

"But Papa would be satisfied," Gilby countered, "and with all of her experience in the stillroom and in the laboratory, Calista must know the means to do so."

"You are both of you outrageous," Amethyst said with a yawn, "and I've no mood for it this morning. Let Calista be. She is meant to be a spinster, I daresay, and I, for one, shall not complain to have a sister who is free to come help out with my children."

This, however, was too much for Mrs. Standish. "Amethyst! How can you wish such a fate upon your sister?" she demanded incredulously.

Xanthe, who had been watching the proceedings with much interest, now asked innocently, "But what about the vicar? Why doesn't Cal marry him?"

Five pairs of eyes turned upon the thirteen-year-old girl. None of the Standish offspring felt quite able to speak, and it was left to Mrs. Standish to reply, in measured tones. "My dear Xanthe, you have evidently overheard a certain amount of discussion concerning Mr. Forster. If so, you must also have overheard enough to know your father's views upon the matter. He is quite unsuitable."

"But why didn't Papa like Mr. Forster?" Xanthe persisted. "He likes Calista and if you are worried that she won't be married in time or that she shall be an old maid—"

"Oh, Xanthe!" Raynor said in patent exasperation. "You don't understand anything."

In a most unladylike manner but very much like the thirteen-year-old she was, Xanthe stuck out her tongue at her brother and said, "How can I understand if no one ever explains anything to me?"

At which point Calista took pity on her younger sister. With a tiny sigh she put an arm about Xanthe's shoulder and said soothingly, "Never mind. Mr. Forster would not do for me, but you cannot be blamed for wondering why."

"Nothing to wonder about," Raynor retorted with a snort. "The man's a cabbage head. And even with the terms of Papa's will, Cal ain't that desperate!"

Amabel Standish eyed her second son with a quelling stare and he fell silent. Then, looking about the morning room at all her offspring, Mrs. Standish was hard put to suppress a sigh. Five children, and her husband so mistaken in naming four of them. He had named Amethyst assuming that she would have the violet eyes that the Standish family was known for. She did not. He had named Calista hoping that she would have her mother's fair hair and coloring and her father's height. She did not. Gilby was tall but also brown-haired rather than fair, as his name would suggest. And he was the one who was military-mad, not his brother Raynor, whose name meant mighty army. Only with Xanthe had he been successful. She was indeed a fair-haired beauty, with violet eyes and a sweet nature.

What, Amabel Standish wondered with a sigh, was she to do with such a brood? To be sure, Mr. Standish had not been a man to ever attend much to practical matters, but somehow a word from him had always been sufficient to quiet the children, even at their noisiest. In so many ways she would miss this man who had so often been so exasperating in life.

The look upon her mother's face did not escape Calista and she made haste to quiet her brothers, who were still quarreling with Xanthe. Amethyst, quick to follow her younger sister's lead, offered to go upstairs with Xanthe to look at some pattern books she had brought with her. Upon hearing this boring news, the two boys declared themselves determined to ride out to be certain that the north wall, which needed work, was being properly repaired.

"For depend upon it," Gilby said with unaccustomed seriousness, "they will think that with Papa gone the work can be slackened. We must show them that we mean to carry on as always."

With an abstracted air that had gradually become a part of her since her husband's death, Amabel Standish waved her sons toward the door.

When her siblings were gone, Calista hesitated several minutes before venturing to speak. At last, however, her mother noticed her and said, with some surprise, "Oh, are you still here, Calista?"

"Yes, Mama," Calista replied patiently. "I wanted to ask you about Mr. Leverton. You said that you had a letter from him."

With an effort Mrs. Standish roused herself from her lethargy and was once more the energetic woman Calista recalled so well. "Yes, and you are right to recall me to the matter. Mr. Leverton writes that he expects to arrive by the end of this week, though in fact he could arrive at any time. The letter took an unconscionable amount of time in reaching me, in spite of Mr. Ralph Allen's new system of the mails. It was supposed to have arrived last week, I gather, and when he wrote, Mr. Leverton was not altogether certain what day he would set out."

Amabel Standish paused thoughtfully for a moment before she added, "We must have Mrs. Hastings make up the green room for Mr. Leverton. He writes that he is not bringing his wife but is bringing a friend, so she must make up the red room as well. The larder is sufficiently well stocked, of that I am persuaded, but I do hope Mr. Leverton and his friend will not expect to be entertained."

"Mama," Calista said gently, "I am sure they will understand we are still in mourning. Indeed, they can scarcely forget it since that is why Mr. Leverton is coming here and he will see all of us dressed in black." Calista paused, then added dryly, "It is just as well Mr. Leverton is already married. In planning as he did, Papa did not allow for how dreadful I look in black."

"Even if he had realized it," her mother said with a wistful smile, "he would have said that any man of sense would discount such a minor consideration. Which I suppose is true of Mr. Leverton, since your father took a fancy to him. But I wonder what his friend's opinion will be, Calista," Mrs. Standish said anxiously.

"Oh, Mama, what can it signify?" Calista answered impatiently. "No doubt he is married as well."

"Ten to one you are right," Mrs. Standish replied sadly, "but one may hope. And if he is not, one must put one's best foot forward."

"Why is this friend coming anyway? There wasn't anyone but Mr. Leverton named in the will, was there?" Calista asked crossly.

Mrs. Standish shrugged. "I really don't know," she said honestly. "I can only suppose that they will be stopping here on their way to somewhere else."

"Or perhaps," Calista suggested, her eyes dancing impishly, "Mr. Leverton does not care to trust himself to a den of strangers alone."

"Calista!" Mrs. Standish remonstrated, a note of despair in her voice. "When will you learn to curb your tongue? It was bad enough when your father was alive and you were a child, but now it is impossible. You must recollect that you are a young lady. It is your father's fault, of course," she said, in the familiar refrain. "Why he had to treat you as though you were a boy when he had two sons, one of them a perfectly acceptable scholar himself, I shall never understand."

Calista's eyes were still dancing as she replied, "Yes, but Mama, Raynor likes books, not fiddling in the laboratory mixing things up together as I do. And our other interests do not overlap in the least. Neither of us alone could have kept up with Papa."

"Yes, well, just so long as you are able to behave as a young lady while Mr. Leverton and his friend are here," Mrs. Standish warned her daughter. "If we are ever to have a hope of marrying you off before your birthday we must be particularly careful of your reputation. It would be disastrous if your reputation as a bluestocking should precede you."

For once Calista did not argue but merely said meekly, "Yes, Mama. I shall try to remember. I shan't even show them my laboratory."

Mrs. Standish shuddered. "Please don't say that word," she begged. "Call it a workroom or something." She paused, then added, "And Calista, I think we might begin to move from black to our grays and purples and dark blues or even dark greens while our guests are here. Papa would have understood."

With a tiny sigh of her own, Calista said, "Yes, Mama."

Outside, Raynor and Gilby were laying their own plans. As they rode toward the fence that needed to be repaired, Gilby said coolly, "What are we going to do about Cal?"

"Do about Cal?" Raynor asked with raised eyebrows. "What do you mean, Gil?"

"I mean," Gilby said impatiently, "how are we going to get Cal married before the time is up? And not to the vicar, either."

With a wry grin Raynor said, "Why, look for a possible husband and then help matters along if we can. Don't worry, we'll think of something, Gil. Though I shouldn't be surprised if Cal thinks of something herself. She always did have the quickest mind of all of us."

Curtly, Gilby nodded. Then, grimly, he added, "Well, at any rate, while he is here I shall ask Mr. Leverton if he will speak to Mama for me, about letting me purchase a pair of colors. We've the money for it, I know we do, and it's only the most absurd scruples that prevent such a venture."

"Oh, aye, absurd," Raynor agreed with a cheerful grin. "Such as the fact that you are the inheritor of this estate and that it will be your duty to settle down and manage it as soon as you come of age."

"Fustian!" Gilby retorted with a snort of disgust. "That is just what I mean. Everyone knows you would be a far better hand at it than I, but because I was born before you were we are not allowed to switch places. I daresay Mama would buy you colors in a trice."

"Now that is where you are out," Raynor replied, more serious this time. "You know that her reasons are at least partly a fear for your safety."

"My safety?" Gilby demanded incredulously, twisting in the saddle to look at his younger brother. "But we are at peace! What danger can there be if we are at peace?"

Raynor studied the mane of his bay stallion as he replied carefully, "Yes, but you are hoping we won't stay at peace, aren't you? Otherwise, what point is there in purchasing colors? You'll find a way to put yourself in the thick of things if you get in the military. Even if it's someone else's thick of things. And what's more, Mama knows it." Gilby did not bother to deny the charge and, after a moment, Raynor went on, "Besides, Mr. Leverton isn't really coming here to look after us, or take on any such responsibilities. He's just fulfilling the terms of Papa's will as gracefully as he can and won't stay above half a day, I should think. He won't be wanting to be bothered by a halfling like you."

Gilby turned a sardonic look upon his younger brother. "Halfling?" he asked. "And what does that make you?"

Raynor shrugged and replied cheerfully, "Even more of a nuisance, I suppose. But at least I don't mean to plague the fellow with things that are none of his business. The man doesn't even know us!"

"I don't mean to plague Mr. Leverton!" Gilby said hotly. It was Raynor's turn to look sardonic and after a moment Gilby said meekly, "Well, not very much, at any rate. I just want him to explain to Mama how it is for a fellow and why I should be allowed to join the military. And he is, after all, supposed to offer her advice about us."

"And suppose he agrees with Mama?" Raynor asked with a grin.

"It's worth a try," Gilby said grimly. "And what other chance have I got, anyway? Papa may have had windmills in his head to appoint the fellow a sort of guardian to us, but he did, so Leverton must make Mama see reason." Then, with a hint of desperation in his voice he added, "Leverton's got to understand how it is."

With a sigh Raynor said, "I hope so, Gil, I hope so."

Some time later, George Trumble was cheerfully walking back to the Standish household after spending a most pleasant afternoon at a nearby tavern. It was, he reflected, pausing at the side of the road before crossing it to cut through some more fields, fortunate that he had found such congenial company there, for Amethyst was not, these days, the pleasantest of companions. Indeed, were his own nature not so easy-going, he might have gone so far as to say that she was showing a distinct tendency toward shrewishness. Instead, he told himself, and others, that the poor thing was feeling markedly peckish, what with breeding and all. Nothing that nine months wouldn't fix. Though he did devoutly hope it wouldn't take quite that long.

Mr. Trumble was still standing there at the side of the road, lost in thought and feeling the pleasant haze of the many pints he had consumed, when a curricle pulled up beside him and two gentlemen looked down at him. The one driving cleared his throat and said in a friendly way, "Excuse me, sir, but can you tell me where I can find the Standish estate?"

Mr. Trumble looked the two men over carefully. They looked to be ten years younger than himself and were dressed in a far more fashionable manner. These were not country fellows but come straight from London, Trumble thought. And then he recalled that Amethyst's mother was expecting some guests. Furthermore, he recalled, it involved old Oliver Standish's will.

3

JOHN WITTON LOOKED down from his curricle at the fellow standing by the side of the road. He noted that the man was of moderate height and portly build, with sandy brown hair, and was some years older than himself and Leverton. The fellow had not answered the question, however, and Witton began to wonder if his wits were wanting. "Hallo," Witton repeated, in the same friendly way, "can you tell me how to get to the Standish estate?"

Hastily, Trumble collected his alcohol-impaired thoughts and replied, "Forgive me. I was woolgathering, I fear. The Standish place is just down this road. Not more than half a mile and to the right. Going that way, myself. George Trumble, sirs, at your service."

He executed a neat bow that nevertheless betrayed his inebriated state, and both Witton and Leverton managed half bows in their seats. Witton introduced both of them to Trumble, then added, "I believe we are expected. Would you care to ride with us the rest of the way? It will be a trifle crowded, but I think we might manage."

Trumble smiled happily. "Don't mind if I do," he said, clambering up. "Lovely little pubs hereabouts, but the devil of a walk from m'wife's home. She's a Standish, too, y'know. The eldest daughter, Amethyst."

"I see," Witton said grimly, as the smell of alcohol reached him where he sat.

"Do you, er, live with your wife's family, then?" Leverton asked gingerly.

Trumble sighed heavily. "Not in the ordinary course of things," he confided. "But m'wife's father died recently and we came for the funeral. Then she began feeling a trifle poorly and we've stayed longer than we originally intended."

Leverton nodded sympathetically. "No wonder you've sought out the local pubs," he said. "Whenever we go to visit my wife's family, I feel inclined to do much the same thing."

Turning to John Witton, Trumble said, "And you, sir, are you married as well?"

Witton shook his head curtly and Leverton answered for him, a distinct twinkle in his eyes as he said, "No, John is a hardened case, I fear. I despair of ever seeing him settled and with a family. He has far too serious a turn of mind to please the ladies, nor will he cultivate the air of a dandy as I have begged him to. All he has to recommend him is a fortune and excellent breeding."

"Well, he'll no doubt please Miss Calista, then," Trumble said with a short laugh. "A more serious female I've never met. Unnatural, that's what it is, for a female to be so concerned with books and science and learning and such. Thank heavens my Amethyst is a proper woman at least."

"Good God, is Miss Standish such an antidote, then?" Leverton asked. "Has she a squint and spectacles and a bookish air about her?"

Abruptly, Trumble appeared to become aware of his indiscretion and hastily tried to undo the damage. "Shouldn't have said that. Hasn't a squint or spectacles," Trumble allowed handsomely. Then, once more, his feelings betrayed him as he added, "I will say, though, there are few lads hereabouts who would have the courage to court her."

"I do not see why a young lady must be castigated for wishing to improve her mind," Witton said stiffly. "I find it admirable."

Mischief filled Leverton's eyes as he said to Witton, "Are you volunteering, John? Have a care or you'll sweep the young lady off her feet with your gallantry and then where will you be."

Now Trumble was distinctly alarmed and he said, "Gentlemen, please! You forget she *is* m'wife's sister, after all. And, in any event, we're here. Just up this lane and we'll find ourselves at the front door and someone will come to take care of the horses. Mind you, don't be put off by the sight of the house. Looks as if it grew bit by bit, wing by wing, rather than being planned. Which in fact is what happened. They say that the oldest part dates to the thirteenth or fourteenth century, and I don't doubt it a bit. But here, don't let that alarm you! Word of honor, the place is perfectly comfortable." He paused, frowned, and then added, "I say, where is your baggage? Can't come visiting without baggage."

"Coming in another carriage, along with our valets," Witton replied coolly.

"Delightful a way as my man has with my clothes, John cannot abide his conversation for hours on end," Leverton added with a grin. "So we came on ahead and left them to follow. I expect we'll see them before the afternoon is out. It would cut my man's soul to the quick if he thought I should be forced to sit down to dinner in my traveling clothes or to dress without his expert help."

"I wish I could convince my man of that," Trumble said with a distinct grimace. "He is forever haring off just when I need him most. And he has the worst way with a boot that I have ever seen."

"Why don't you just turn him off, then?" Witton asked sensibly.

"Turn him off?" Trumble asked, astonished, as he dismounted from the curricle. "How can I? His father was my father's valet and his father's father was my grandfather's man. One just doesn't turn off a family retainer that way. Besides, there ain't anyone better I can find," he added, rather spoiling the effect of his neat little speech.

"Pardon me, I stand corrected," Witton murmured as Leverton also dismounted the vehicle.

Trumble looked at him sharply, but Witton's face was all innocence and Trumble contented himself with calling to the groom who had appeared from around the corner of the house to hurry along and take the reins. Only when the fellow had done so did Witton climb down and then all three mounted the steps to the house. They had scarcely reached the door when it was opened by a young girl.

A trifle embarrassed, Trumble said, "Xanthe! What the devil are you doing answering the door? That's what the servants are for."

"I know, but I couldn't wait to see who was here," she replied ingenuously.

Trumble snorted disapprovingly, then said, "I shall speak to your mother later about your harum-scarum manners, young lady. Is she about? Mr. Leverton and Mr. Witton have just arrived from London."

"I knew it!" the girl said eagerly. "I saw you from the window and I knew it had to be them. I'll get Mama straightaway."

Then, true to her word, the girl fled, leaving Trumble to lead the two gentlemen forward to the small parlor that served as a drawing room. As he did so, a very embarrassed footman took their hats. "I'll inform Mrs. Standish you are here," he said hastily.

As he spoke, Mrs. Standish appeared, hurrying forward to greet them. "Mr. Trumble! Xanthe tells me you have brought our guests. Mr. Leverton, I presume? I am Mrs. Standish, Oliver Standish's widow."

Freddy bowed and then said, "May I present my good friend, John Witton?"

Witton bowed and Mrs. Standish inclined her head in his direction before she turned back to Freddy and said, "I trust you had no trouble finding us, Mr. Leverton?"

It cannot be denied that Witton was a trifle taken aback by such cavalier treatment. He was, after all, accustomed to being treated with the utmost deference the moment his name was mentioned to mothers of eligible daughters. Incredible as it seemed, Mrs. Standish did not appear to know who he was. Grimly he listened as his friend answered her question.

"Not after we were fortunate enough to encounter Mr. Trumble," Freddy replied. "He directed us and we were here in a trice."

"Well, you are very welcome," Mrs. Standish said warmly. "I know this whole journey must be an irksome task for you, but we shall try to make you feel at home. Won't you come into the drawing room and have something to refresh yourself while I see to it that Mrs. Hastings has your rooms ready? I am expecting the girl to bring the tea tray at any moment, but if you prefer I can have Matthews fetch some wine. I am not a connoisseur, but everyone tells me that my late husband laid down an extraordinarily fine collection of wine.''

"He certainly did," Trumble confirmed with a happy smile, "as did his father before him."

"Tea will be fine," Leverton said calmly.

Trumble looked a trifle disappointed but did not object. Neither did Witton. Mrs. Standish smiled and led them the rest of the short way to the drawing room, arriving just after the girl with the tea tray and at the same moment as a young woman who had an abstracted air about her.

It was quite evident, Witton thought with an inward smile, that no one had thought to warn the young lady that there were visitors for she wore a black cloth gown with an apron over it that had clearly been designed with practicality rather than fashion in mind. Her hair, moreover, had been bundled up haphazardly onto the top of her head and a great many tendrils were beginning to escape their pins, and even now she seemed scarcely aware of the two men.

In this, Witton was mistaken. Calista was very much aware of her mother's visitors. And she felt fully the mortification of being caught out in such an unbecoming dress. But she would not let them see it. Instead, unconsciously tilting her chin up, she said, a trifle breathlessly, "Mama, there's a problem with the laundry. It seems the boys have been putting dead rats in the wash water again."

Mrs. Standish rolled her eyes skyward, as

though in a silent prayer, then sighed and said, "I suppose Mrs. Pennyworth is having hysterics, as usual?"

Calista nodded. Reluctantly, Mrs. Standish turned to her guests and said, "Mr. Leverton, Mr. Witton, my daughter Calista. Make your curtsy, child." She paused, then went on, "You will excuse us, I know. Xanthe, pour the gentlemen some tea. And you come with me," she told Calista sternly.

As they walked away from the drawing room the two women could hear Trumble's voice saying, "Told you the girl was an odd one."

Mrs. Standish's lips pressed into a thinner line than ever, and as soon as they were well away from the drawing room she stopped and turned to her daughter. "Calista, you are to go upstairs at once and change into your prettiest mourning gown. I will deal with the wash," she added hastily to forestall her daughter's protest. "Right now you must change and then go and entertain our guests. I will not have them going away agreeing with George Trumble that you are an odd one!"

"Yes, Mama," Calista said. Then, gently, she added, "Any suitor for my hand must learn to take me as I am, Mama, for I do not think I could pretend to anything else."

Mrs. Standish did not even bother to answer, but sighed and then said in a martyred voice, "I wonder if Mrs. Pennyworth has fainted yet?"

Calista watched her mother go in the direction

of the wash houses, then she obediently went upstairs to change her dress. No more than her mother did she wish the world to see her as eccentric. The trouble was, it seemed extraordinarily difficult not to have it do so. Papa's attitude had always been that it was the world and not Oliver or Calista Standish who was at fault, and while she did not entirely agree, she felt helpless to change matters in the least.

Once in her room she reached unhesitatingly for the mauve muslin gown with black trim that became her so well. A few deft touches with a brush and the proper placement of pins and Calista might have been mistaken for any of the delightfully dressed young ladies of leisure that filled the drawing rooms and ballrooms in London during the Season. She might not be a beauty, Calista told herself calmly, but Mama should have no cause now to be ashamed of her. She would, she resolved, restrain her tongue for as long as she could do so.

It was therefore an apparently demure young lady who joined the gentlemen from London and George Trumble as they were finishing their tea. To Leverton's pleasant surprise and Witton's scarcely acknowledged disappointment, Calista even contrived to sound no different from any other young lady of their acquaintance. But only for a short time.

The image was shattered when Gilby and Raynor burst into the room, almost breathless, demanding that their sister settle an argument. To be sure, they allowed her to introduce them to the gentlemen from London, but then began to hammer at her with their questions.

"Who was it lost the Swedish territories to Russia, Poland, and Denmark?" Raynor demanded hotly.

"I told you, it was Ulrica Eleanora," Gilby said impatiently before Calista could answer. "They made her promise not to fight before they let her on the throne."

"But it was Charles the Twelfth's folly that led to it," Raynor retorted.

Calmly, Calista replied, "Actually, it was during Ulrica's reign that most of the losses did occur. But Raynor is quite right that Charles the Twelfth's insistence on hounding the king of Poland set the stage for revenge. Still, had he not so successfully defended Sweden against the Danes, Poles, and Russians they would have entirely carved up his kingdom when they formed a league against him in seventeen hundred."

"Are you sure?" Gilby asked suspiciously. "I thought that alliance came later, under Ulrica."

"Of course she's sure," Raynor retorted contemptuously. "Have you ever known Cal to be wrong?"

As the boys left the room, still deep in their discussion of Swedish history, Calista turned tranquilly to her mother's guests. "Papa always insisted we learn the world's history, not just

England's,' she explained, and then went back to talking about the weather.

George Trumble looked at Leverton and Witton as though to say "I told you so," but Witton was too engrossed in his own thoughts to notice.

Generally accounted too sober a fellow, most of Witton's acquaintances would have been astonished to see that as he looked at Calista Standish, a smile began to twitch the corners of his mouth upward and his eyes began to dance as merrily as Leverton's ever had. A circumstance that was not lost upon his friend. With his own smile of satisfaction, Leverton watched as Witton abruptly entered the conversation and said, "Miss Standish, I understand your father was something of a scholar. Was there anything he was particularly interested in?"

For the first time a genuine smile animated Calista's features as she replied with a laugh, "Everything! From the sciences to history to the arts. I sometimes think that Papa's only failing was that he had no ear for music, but even so he was interested in the science of making instruments."

"Some would call it an art," Witton observed mildly.

Again Calista smiled. "Yes, but you could never have gotten Papa to agree to that. He was convinced that everything could be reduced to science, one way or another. He even tried to decipher the Rosetta Stone with varous mathematical approaches. Had he not died when he did, I think he might very well have succeeded."

There was a slight catch in her throat as she said this but Witton tactfully ignored it and asked, "Was he acquainted with Dr. Thomas Young?"

Calista laughed. "Dr. Young and he corresponded for some time, in sharp disagreement. Then there was Champollion, the Frenchman. Papa wrote to him as well. And Lenoir and, oh, a dozen others. It was his greatest frustration that he could not announce success first. But he was still working on it when he died. He said the others had made a start and he would make the finish if he could."

"I would like to have met your father," Witton said with quiet sincerity. "And I wish I could have seen his work on the Rosetta Stone."

"You can," Calista said immediately. "Papa's notes are still in his library and he always told me that he hoped that scholars would come, after his death, to look at his work. Come, I'll show you."

As she rose to her feet, Witton did also. "You will excuse us?" he asked Leverton and Trumble and Xanthe.

"Unless you wish to come as well," Calista offered generously.

Trumble hastily shook his head. "Above m'touch, m'dear."

"Mine as well," Leverton said with patent amusement. "You two go along. We shall be quite comfortable here."

After only a moment's hesitation, they did so.

4

THE LIBRARY, JOHN Witton thought, truly reflected the mind of its owner. It was a small room, lined with bookcases that were built right into the walls, and filled with a hodgepodge of furniture ranging from conventional to a stool that Calista explained came from a South Sea island. Upon the mantel of the fireplace and all about the room were odd bits of statues or pieces of natural substances and even a few exotic plants. The paintings that hung on the wall, moreover, were a mixture of the familiar and the exotic as well. Prominently displayed upon an easel by his desk was a copy of the heiroglyphics known as the Rosetta Stone and beside it the copious notes that Oliver Standish had evidently made before he died.

As John Witton looked about the room, Calista Standish watched him closely, alert for any sign that he meant to laugh at her father. Oliver Standish had been an unusual man, she knew, and there were not a few who called him dotty. Indeed, she had her own quarrels to pick with him, particularly about his will. But Calista had loved her father fiercely, as well, and it was only when Mr. Witton smiled kindly at her that Calista realized how badly she wanted him to understand. And he did. To Calista's surprise, his questions about the Rosetta Stone were intelligent and it was evident that he had more than a passing acquaintance with the work that was being done by others in the field. And she found herself wondering why she had not heard his name before.

Of course, her surprise was as nothing compared to Witton's surprise at the extent of Calista's knowledge. It was quickly apparent that Oliver Standish had enlisted his daughter's abilities in his efforts to unravel the puzzle. "Do you carry on the work now?" he asked after awhile.

Slowly, Calista shook her head. "Not anymore. Papa would be disappointed, I know, but I do not really care for it. I would far rather be pottering about in the library he built for me." She paused and laughed. "First we meant to use Mama's stillroom, but after a particularly disastrous experiment with some strange powders someone sent Papa she banished us forever from any room connected to the house. So now I use one of the outbuildings—when Mama lets me."

The last was said with a troubled frown and without meaning to do so, Witton found himself moving much closer to Calista. With a frown of his own and a warmth he did not hear in his voice, Witton said, "Does your mother then forbid you to experiment, Miss Standish? I cannot credit it! You've too fine a mind to waste."

Calista looked up at Witton, her eyes reflecting the distress she felt. She had not meant to tell this stranger so much, had not even realized how strongly she herself felt about matters until this moment. Or how alone. Oliver and Amabel Standish were affectionate parents when they remembered to be, but Calista had for some time developed the habit of solving problems herself and dealing with matters in her own way. And what could not be changed she had simply accepted. There had, after all, been no one who shared her sentiments so exactly as this stranger seemed to do and for the first time Calista was aware of how lonely she had been for so very long. It was a strange and compelling feeling and perhaps that was why, in the end, she spoke as frankly as she did.

In a voice that was not altogether steady, Calista said, "My mother does not forbid it—not precisely, at any rate. It is just that since Papa died she finds so many things for me to do about the house. And they do need to be done and perhaps I am the best one to do it, but . . ."

"But you cannot help feeling that she wishes to discourage your researches?" Witton asked grimly.

Alarmed by the note of anger in his voice,

Calista answered hastily. "You must not blame Mama, Mr. Witton. She is only concerned about my future. Truly she is. And can you blame her?" Calista turned away, her eyes fixed upon the floor as she said quietly, "I know that I am called an eccentric, a bluestocking, if you will. Known more as the scholar's daughter than by my own name. Mr. Trumble thinks me scarcely a woman. Tells me to my face I should cultivate my needle and my watercolors and cease trying to behave as I am."

"And your mother permits him to speak to you in that way?" Witton demanded, disapproval and shock evident in his voice and on his face.

Briefly, Calista's mischievous smile returned. "Oh, no. If Mama were to hear him she would tell him that what I do is none of his affair and that if he wishes to be welcome in her house he had best not try to tell her daughters what to do!" The smile faded as Calista added, "I haven't told her what he says. It only happens when he comes home from drinking at the pubs hereabouts. And Mama has too much to bear as it is."

"I've half a mind to speak to him myself," Witton said grimly. "He has said more than one thing that I take exception to already."

"Oh, no, you must not!" Calista said at once, reaching out a hand as though to stop him.

"Calista! Mr. Witton!" A shocked voice interrupted them from the doorway of the room.

As one the pair turned to see Mrs. Standish staring at them with appalled eyes. "What on earth is going on in here?" she demanded. "And why did you desert our other guests, Calista? I found Xanthe trying to entertain Mr. Leverton while Mr. Trumble has disappeared heaven knows where!"

Guiltily, Calista flushed, but it was John Witton who answered Mrs. Standish's attack. With a bow he said, in cool tones, "It was my fault, I'm afraid, Mrs. Standish. Your daughter was speaking of her father's work with the Rosetta Stone and I asked to see it. I wished to know if he had followed Young's lead or Champollion's. I am delighted to discover that he used a method all his own."

At this reference to her late husband's work, Mrs. Standish visibly relaxed as she said, "Still, Calista should have chosen another time. You must be tired from your journey and wish to rest a bit before we sit down to dine. We keep country hours, you know. Oh, and I meant to tell you, your valet has arrived with your things. We have put you in the red room; it is at the end of this hall."

Witton allowed a trifle more warmth to creep into his voice as he bowed again and said, "Thank you, Mrs. Standish. And you, Miss Standish, for allowing me to see your father's work. But I must not keep you any longer."

With a final bow he strode from the room, leaving Calista to finger the locket at her throat as she faced her mother. The last words he heard, ones that set a grim line to Witton's lips, were, "And just what were you telling Mr. Witton he must not do, Calista?"

In the room given over to his use, Witton found his friend Leverton lounging on the bed with an insufferably smug expression on his face. "Well?" Leverton demanded.

"Well, what?" Witton said shortly.

"Come, come, John, tell me what you think of Standish's daughter," Leverton retorted impatiently.

"Miss Xanthe? I found her charmingly pretty and impetuous," Witton replied, turning away and pretending to adjust his cravat in the mirror.

"Careful," Leverton said with a laugh. "If you crumple your neckcloth any more than that your man will never forgive you. And I shall not be dissuaded anyway. I mean to know what you think of Miss Calista."

Witton turned to face his friend. "First," he said grimly, "let us talk about you. What were you about, telling Trumble I am unattached? I thought we agreed to pretend I was not. I've no intention of becoming a matchmaker's target here as well as in London, Freddy. Particularly as these people do not seem to know who I am."

Leverton sighed. "You're right. I had forgotten. Look, I'll take care of the matter at dinner. But for now, *I* want to know what you think of Miss Standish."

With a laugh Witton replied, "You are incorrigible! Very well, Freddy," he said, "I found Miss Calista intelligent, with a surprisingly well-informed mind, and I cannot help wondering what windmills Oliver Standish must have had in his head if he ever thought you and his daughter would suit!" He paused and added impatiently, "Now what the devil are you grinning at?"

"You," Leverton replied easily, still stretched out on Witton's bed, hands behind his head. "I haven't seen you this animated over a lady since Maria. And after her I thought neither of us would ever have that look again."

"Yes, well, Miss Calista is nothing like Maria ever was," Witton replied shortly.

"True, the Standish chit lacks Maria's astonishing beauty and sparkle and wit and—" Leverton said smoothly.

"I meant," Witton said, ruthlessly cutting short his friend, "that Miss Calista lacks Maria's arrogance and callousness and tendencies toward melodrama. One cannot conceive of Miss Calista fainting because a mouse has crossed *her* path, or threatening to go into a decline because one has not come to call more than thrice in two days, or running merrily from one beau to another as the whim takes her."

"That's because she hasn't got the beaux to do so," Leverton said frankly, "and one can easily see why."

In an instant Witton was standing over his friend, clenched fists by his side. "What I see is a woman with more to recommend her than any of the mindless chits one finds at Almack's! So don't speak to me of beauty. As for wit, I should think Miss Calista's would wear far better day after day, year after year, over the breakfast table than Maria's." he told Leverton roundly.

"Peace, John," Leverton said laughing and playfully putting out his hands as if to ward off a blow. "Can't you tell when I am roasting you?"

With a shaky laugh of his own, Witton backed away a step and said, "No, I cannot. And in any event, it was not kind of you, Freddy, if you were."

"No, nor wise I begin to think," Leverton agreed, sitting up. "I had no notion you were so ready with your fists to defend a lady's honor."

Witton moved to stand by the window, looking out through the thick panes of glass. After a moment's pause he said, "No, nor I. But there is something about Miss Standish that makes one want to defend her and protect her as evidently no one in her family has ever done. Do you know her mother has tried to discourage her researches?"

"Astonishing!" Leverton murmured.

Witton looked at his friend. "Oh, do give over," he said shortly. "I know you do not think research a fit occupation for a woman. And that Mrs. Standish only wishes to see her daughter properly wed which, to her, constitutes happiness. But for someone with a mind like Miss Standish has, that is tantamount to sentencing her real self to death. I cannot stand by and see that occur."

With raised eyebrows, Leverton asked his friend soberly, "And how do you mean to stop it? Short of marrying the girl yourself, what do you imagine you can do?"

Witton did not at once answer. Finally, a mischievous grin lit up his face and eyes as he replied, "I begin to think, Freddy, that I shall have to cultivate my skills as a diplomat and convince Mrs. Standish that her daughter is far more marketable as a rare *objet d'art*, or rather *objet de science*, of course, than as a run-of-the-mill young thing making her comeout."

Arms crossed over his chest, a matching smile upon his own face, Leverton said, "Now this I am going to enjoy. I have seen you in many guises and do not doubt your abilities, but even for you this is going to be a challenge. You had best hope that Mrs. Standish takes a liking to you or the case is lost from the start."

Meanwhile, Mrs. Standish and Calista were still in the library. Mrs. Standish had had a great many questions of her own. "What was he doing?" she repeated after Mr. Witton had left the room. "He must have been trying to take some sort of liberties with you or you wouldn't have been telling him to stop. No, nor reaching out to place your hand on his chest!" she added roundly.

Coloring and avoiding her mother's eyes Calista replied, "He was taking no liberties, I assure you. It was something to do with my work and Papa's."

"*Your* work?" Mrs. Standish echoed ominously. "You have no work, Calista, except to find a husband and be married. And you will seriously harm your chances of doing so if you behave as you did today. How could you go off alone with him? Unchaperoned? A man you have just met today?"

"I was showing him Papa's work," Calista said evenly. "He asked to see it."

"That is no excuse," her mother said haughtily. "It was still improper to come here with him along. You should have brought Xanthe and Mr. Leverton as well."

"They weren't interested," Calista replied, still evenly.

Recognizing the stubborn tilt of her daughter's chin, Mrs. Standish turned away, resignation evident in every movement. With a tiny sigh she said, her voice quivering with concern, "I do not know what Mr. Witton must have thought of you. It should have been your brother's place, either of them, to show your father's work to Mr. Witton. But no, you had to do so yourself. It is my fault, of course. I should never have allowed your father to corrupt you so, but I could never deny him anything. Now he is gone and you don't know how to behave as a young lady and every gentleman who sees you goes away shaking his head over the unnatural female."

"You are mistaken, Mama," Calista said with quiet dignity. "Mr. Witton respects my mind and finds nothing unnatural about it. Indeed, he encouraged me to continue my researches."

Mrs. Standish sniffed, her back still toward her daughter. "Why not?" she asked aloud. "Is it his concern if you find a husband? And by your twenty-first birthday, at that? Does he care if you are doomed to spinsterhood all your life? Does he know or care how blighted your life will be without a hearth and children of your own to care for? Or did he say so in hopes of encouraging you to behave improperly? In hopes that you would place your hand on his chest and behave in heaven knows what other brazen manner? To think that my Calista could so far forget herself with a stranger!"

Mrs. Standish broke off with a small sob. Calista, however, was not daunted. Indeed, a smile began to turn up the corners of her mouth and dimple her cheeks as she said innocently, "Do you mean, Mama, that it would have been all right if I had known him better? If Mr. Witton had not been a stranger, but some gentleman I knew well?"

Mrs. Standish whirled around in shocked horror and said, "Certainly not, Calista!" Then, seeing her daughter's impish expression she threw up her hands. "Oh, very well, I shan't chide you any longer. You know what occurred and I do not. But please, Calista, do try to think of appearances as well. And at dinner, try to behave with perfect propriety. Heaven only knows what Mr. Leverton and his friend think of us already."

"I shall try, Mama," Calista said meekly.

"Good. Meanwhile, I mean to find out if Mr. Witton is married," her mother replied grimly. She paused, then added thoughtfully, "Wear your dark blue silk dress for dinner, Calista. It cannot do any harm to look your best, and perhaps something may be salvaged yet."

5

IF JOHN WITTON did not succeed in charming Mrs. Standish immediately, he did at any rate mollify her fears by treating Calista with a distant respect and speaking favorably to Mrs. Standish of her late husband. He then stepped into the background and allowed Frederick Leverton, over dinner, to draw her out in the matter of those of Oliver Standish's affairs that he had been asked to look into. Somewhat to Leverton's surprise, they were in exceedingly good order.

"That is to Mama's credit," Calista interjected. "She has always had all control of the household accounts. Although Papa did give the orders concerning the home farm. He had so many ideas he wanted to try out, you see."

"And my husband was meticulous about keeping records for everything, whether it was a financial matter, real estate, or family business," Mrs. Standish added proudly. "He always said that if one did these things right an absolute stranger could step in and know at once what was what."

"How fortunate," Witton said dryly.

"Yes, wasn't it," George Trumble said brightly.

"Considering the circumstances and all. Not much use denying you are a stranger, Mr. Leverton."

Wary of her son-in-law's tongue, Mrs. Standish hastily drew Gilby into the discussion. "In any event, my eldest son, Gilby, would no doubt have been able to answer most of your questions. My husband believed in keeping Gilby well informed on all matters concerning the estate, starting when he was quite young."

Mrs. Standish beamed proudly at her eldest son, who promptly snorted and said, "Gammon, Mama! Raynor understands it all far better than I do, as well you know. Which is why you ought to buy me colors and let him continue on with learning about the estate."

Beside him Raynor gave a snort of his own and said softly, "You gudgeon, Gil! Must you always rush your fences?"

Fortunately, no one but Gilby overheard Raynor as Mrs. Standish was engaged in loudly informing her son that she would never purchase colors for him. "Your father was against it, Gilby, and how you can ask me to go against his sacred wishes is more than I can fathom. It would have broken his heart to hear you talk this way. You know that he always said that if you did not wish to run the estate he would understand if you chose to go to Oxford or Cambridge instead."

"But I don't want to go to Oxford or Cambridge and be a scholar," Gilby said through gritted teeth. "As for breaking Papa's heart, that's nonsense. I told him to his face how I felt. And just because he couldn't understand doesn't mean you never should!"

Gilby rose to make a dramatic exit, but Witton's voice acted like a dash of cold water in the face as he said, "I am astonished at how at home you are contriving to make us feel, Mrs. Standish. I can remember just such a conversation when my younger brother wanted to join up just after Napoleon escaped from Elba. Of course," he added apologetically, "it was a trifle easier for my mother as my brother was younger than Gilby and suffering from the measles at the time. Between the two, the battle at Waterloo had taken place by the time Edwin could have obtained a commission."

"He's well enough now, isn't he?" Gilby demanded impatiently.

"And old enough," Witton agreed, "but since the war is over he's lost interest, I'm afraid. It was the French, particularly, that he wanted to fight, you see."

With a sigh Gilby said, "I wish *I* could have been at Waterloo! It must have been something extraordinary."

"It was," Leverton said grimly. "Extraordinarily wet and cold and deadly."

"Were you there, then?" Gilby asked eagerly.

Leverton nodded grimly. "We both were," he said, "though John can tell the tale better than I."

As he fell silent Witton began to speak. "We

weren't in the midst of the fighting, of course, but we were in Brussels at the time. And I still remember the carts of wounded streaming the streets red with blood. And the other wounded thrown over horses because that was the only way to get them out of the battle. I remember the dead and dying, the mass graves, and the horror of men maimed for the rest of their lives."

"It was a victory," Leverton added as Witton stopped speaking. "But a victory that claimed far too many lives, far too many friends, for any of us who were near there to think of it as a time of glory."

Abashed, Gilby fell silent leading Amabel Standish to favor him with a triumphant look. George Trumble cleared his throat and said, "There, you see, Gilby? Your Mama was quite right to forbid talk of purchasing colors."

Which in turn led Raynor to take up the cudgels in his brother's behalf. "But look, it isn't always that way, is it?" Raynor asked anxiously.

Witton took pity on the boy. "No, it isn't always that way," he agreed, a slight twinkle in his eyes. "But you'd best ask Mr. Leverton about that. He has a brother-in-law who was an aide-de-camp to the Duke of Wellington himself. And who is still in the military, for that matter."

"Really?" Gilby asked, once more heartened.

"Really," Leverton confirmed. "Colonel Jason Milford. And he would say that whatever the risks, it can be a place for a young lad to grow into a man and also to do a service for his country." He then turned to Mrs. Standish and said, "I know very well that I am *not* in a position to judge what is best for Gilby, whatever your husband's will might have said. But should you ever change your mind I should be happy to give Gilby my brother's direction and to recommend the boy's career to his notice."

All but awestruck, Gilby managed a husky, "Thank you."

Amabel Standish was not nearly so pleased. Bristling a trifle she said, "That is extremely kind of you, Mr. Leverton. As I am most unlikely to change my mind, however, I doubt Gilby will have the need to impose upon you in such a way. As for what you and Mr. Witton must think of us, arguing in front of you in this manner . . ."

Her gaze included both guests, and with a gallant smile Witton said, "I have already told you, it has made us feel at home, and that is no small thing, I assure you! If all families were as frank and forthright as yours with strangers, how much more comfortable we would all be."

Trumble looked at Witton in patent disbelief, but Amabel Standish managed a tremulous smile. "You are very kind," she said.

Xanthe, who had been watching everything with great interest, and Amethyst, who was feeling distinctly unwell, could only silently but fervently agree. As for Calista, she felt a smile begin to creep into her own eyes and tug at her mouth. Never before had she seen anyone besides Papa so neatly handle Mama. It was one more reason for her to feel a grateful warmth toward Mr. Witton. She cringed inwardly, however, at her mother's next words.

"Are you married, Mr. Witton?" Mrs. Standish asked forthrightly.

A number of sudden coughs were heard about the table as John replied in a somewhat strangled voice, "No, Mrs. Standish, I am not."

"But his affections are attached," Leverton added hastily, recognizing all too well the thunderous look on his friend's face.

Astonished, Trumble said, "But you said earlier you despaired of him ever becoming attached to anyone!"

There were more strangled coughs and a number of people changed color rapidly, but finally Leverton recovered sufficiently to say, "It is a circumstance John confided to me only just this afternoon. After we spoke with you. I had not known it, but the attachment is longstanding and being kept quiet for the moment because . . . because . . ."

Wearily, Witton came to his rescue. "Because there are family difficulties. Her parents wish an elder sister wed first and that may take some time."

Mrs. Standish, who had realized too late the enormity of what she had done, now made haste to smooth things over herself. "I meant to ask, you see, whether, if you were married, your own family meals were as . . . as chaotic as ours. But I don't express myself very well, I fear. Now Raynor, he has a way with words."

"Indeed he does," Trumble agreed. "Not but what I should rather see him on a horse. Still he does very well with words. Wrote a first-class poem when Amethyst and I were married. Didn't understand a word of it, but I assure you it was first class."

With the conversation safely diverted, everyone breathed something of a sigh of relief.

After dinner, the ladies withdrew. When it became clear that Gilby and Raynor meant to stay at the table, however, George Trumble cleared his throat and said to them with a frown, "You may go, boys. No one will expect you to hang about."

"But we don't want to go!" Gilby replied, a stubborn set to his jaw.

"Now, now," Trumble said condescendingly, "these gentlemen won't want to be pestered about Waterloo or about purchasing your colors. And I collect that is what you mean to do."

"I don't," Raynor said quietly. "I mean to ask them about the universities. Calista says that Mr. Witton must be familiar with the best men at both Cambridge and Oxford because of how much he knew when he visited Papa's study."

Witton permitted himself a small smile and there was something of a twinkle in his eyes as he said gravely, "Not quite all the best men. In fact, I am a mere dilettante, a dabbler compared to your father, who was a true scholar. Surely he could have told you whatever you wished to know?"

Raynor hesitated a moment and Gilby answered for him. "Papa didn't approve of Raynor's plans. He wants to be a writer, you see, and Papa considered writers, well, rather useless."

"When I told him I wanted to be a poet, he all but threatened to disown me!" Raynor burst out aggrievedly. "Unless they are dead he wants nothing to do with writers."

This time Witton hid his smile as he asked, "What did he want for you, then?"

Hesitantly, Raynor said, "From my name I must think that he once hoped to see me a soldier."

"But he must have realized that wouldn't do," Gilby said scornfully. "What he did admit to was hoping that Raynor would become a scientist or an engineer or even a historian. Anything *useful*, as he called it. That's what he wanted for me, as well. Only Raynor and I aren't suited to those things. Calista might be, but she's a woman, so that's out. In the end, I'm afraid we all disappointed our father."

"Somehow I find that difficult to believe," Witton said quietly. "Those are all estimable fields, but not the only ones worth counting. I am also surprised that your father, if he did indeed entertain notions of Raynor's following the drum, would not be willing to see you do so, Gilby."

"That is what I told their Papa," George

Trumble said heavily, once more entering the fray. "But he would not listen to my advice. Once he got a maggot in his head, nothing could alter it. The man was a brilliant scholar, I would scarcely try to deny it. Indeed, I could not. But as a practical man he was hopeless. One need only look at the matter of his absurd will to see that."

Leverton and Witton avoided each other's eyes and there was an awkward silence before Gilby said, hesitantly, "Would it be plaguing you both too much to ask about Waterloo? I know you said it was horrible, but I would like to hear about it. What really did happen at the battle? And afterward. When Wellington invaded France. Was there much fighting then? What about when he took Paris? Were you there for that?"

Leverton and Witton did their best to answer the boy's questions. Both men found themselves liking the lad's eager intelligence. If he had had a glorified notion of war, he soon grasped what they told him of the realities and it did not damp his interest in the tactics and strategies involved in planning a battle or fighting a war. Nor did he discount the part that chance played in all of it.

Later, when they were alone, Witton found himself observing to Leverton, "What an extraordinary evening!"

"What an extraordinary family, you mean," Leverton countered. "I tried to tell you, John, what you were in for, but I suspect neither of us believed it. I confess I shall be happy to see the last of this unconventional family, however entertaining they may be. Still, young Gilby would make a fine soldier if he can convince his mother to let him join up. England could use officers with minds as sharp as his. I must speak to Jason about the boy."

Ignoring the comments about Gilby, Witton asked with some alarm, "How soon do you mean to leave?"

Leverton shrugged. "I shall stay a full day more. And leave the morning after. I shouldn't wish to insult them by departing as soon as I have arrived, but more than that I should not like to endure. Why, John? Are you not as eager to leave as I?"

It was Witton's turn to shrug. "Oh, I find them all entertaining, as you say. And as I've nowhere particular to go afterward, I am not in such a rush as you." John paused, grinned, then added, "I have not, after all, a wife waiting for me with a new-born child."

Leverton regarded his friend thoughtfully, a great deal passing unspoken between the pair. The urge to roast Witton was strong, but in the end he contented himself with saying quietly, "Actually, John, I was going to ask a favor of you. There are a few matters here which are not so simple to attend to and I thought perhaps you could act in my stead. If that is all right with you and with Mrs. Standish," he added quickly. "You are correct in thinking I am anxious to return to Eleanor. For all that I know she is in good hands, I cannot help but worry over her."

"If it is all right with Mrs. Standish I should be pleased to act in your stead," Witton replied gravely.

"Good," Leverton said, clapping his friend on the shoulder and hiding a smile.

Witton was not deceived, however. "But mind," he said, wagging a finger at Leverton, "I am not going to marry the chit just because Oliver Standish had an absurd notion that you would. I'll confine my help to official matters at hand."

"That's all I ask," Leverton protested with a grin.

"Yes, but is it all that Mrs. Standish will ask?" Witton said aloud.

"After her *faux pas* at dinner I should think Mrs. Standish will be extremely careful not to give offense," Leverton said dryly. "What a blow to your ego that must have been—to discover a matchmaking nother who does not know who you are!" he added with a laugh.

"If so, that is one small thing to be grateful for," Witton answered shortly.

Leverton was still laughing, however, as he went on, "Lord, her face was a study when she realized the commotion she had caused!"

"Are you certain she was not reacting to your absurd explanation?" Witton retorted sardonically.

"Mine?" Leverton asked with mock astonishment. "What about yours? Unmarried elder daughter indeed!"

And at that both men broke into helpless laughter. In a much improved mood, they made plans for the morning, then bade each other good night.

6

THE NEXT MORNING John Witton made a point
of searching out Calista, meaning to apologize for
the trouble that had occurred the day before. He
found her in the old outbuilding that she used as a
laboratory. She was with a most unsavory looking
character.

"Ah, good morning, Mr. Witton," she said as he
entered the doorway, stooping slightly to do so.
"Meet Johnson. He's brought me some samples
from the colony at Australia."

Witton took the cluster of leaves she held out to
him. "Interesting," he said looking them over
carefully. "What are they used for?"

Calista laughed, a becoming animation lighting
up her face as she took them back from him. "I
don't know, precisely. That's the fun of it. Though
I rather think that a mixture of these leaves, bay
leaves, cloves, and perhaps some clover in a bowl
might help keep down the flies. They've a nice
scent as well. And Mr. Curtis, the gentleman who
gave Johnson the leaves to bring me, or rather my
father, sends a note that the natives use them in

various mixtures as a means of treating coughs and congestion. But I shall be extremely careful before trying that."

"I should think so!" Witton said with some surprise.

Calista's eyes took on a determined sparkle as she said coolly, "Do you think, then, that I do not know what I am doing, Mr. Witton? Or that I am not qualified to carry out such experiments?"

"Miss Standish, I have no notion what you are or are not qualified to do," Witton said with a calm smile, "but for anyone to experiment in such a way would require caution, I should think."

"Cured me black cough last time I was here, Miss Calista did," Johnson said, stepping between the pair. "Not a doctor I'd rather have but her treating me if I was ill."

Amusement flickered across Witton's face and Calista was hard put to suppress a smile as she said, gravely, "Thank you, Johnson, but Mr. Witton cannot be expected to have the same faith in me that you have when we have been acquainted only one short day."

"Aye," Johnson said with a curt nod to Calista, "I was just wanting the gentleman to know that I do."

"Thank you," Calista repeated. "But why don't you go up to the kitchen? Mrs. Pennyworth will never forgive me if she doesn't see you while you are here."

With a final look at Witton, Johnson did as he

was bid. When the fellow was gone, Witton turned to Calista and said, "He seems a rough customer, Miss Standish. I am astonished to find you on such friendly terms with him."

Calista smoothed down the unbleached muslin of the apron she wore over her dark green dress as she turned back to the table at which she had been working. Over her shoulder she said, carelessly, "Johnson? Why should I not be on friendly terms with him? He is Mrs. Pennyworth's nephew and grew up hereabouts. I have known him since I was a child. Ten years ago he went to sea, but he always comes back to see us when he can. Usually bringing plants and powders and unusual objects he has come across on his travels. My father was always very grateful to him for doing so. Should I be any less grateful? Particularly as over the years I am the one who has come to benefit? For the two or three years before he died, Papa left the laboratory experiments in my hands."

Abruptly, Calista turned and faced Witton again as she said, "Or do you mean to preach propriety at me?"

"On the contrary," he said stiffly, "I came to beg pardon for being the cause of distress for you yesterday. I should never have pried into your family's affairs. I am not generally in the habit of doing so."

"Nor I of sharing mine with strangers," Calista replied frankly.

There was something in her face that made

Witton say, impulsively, "I wish you will let me speak to Mr. Trumble. I can understand that a certain delicacy of feeling on your part would make it difficult for you to allow that it is my place to do so, but—"

He stopped short as Calista smiled wistfully up at him and then shook her head. "If it should come to that, I am perfectly capable of dealing with my brother-in-law myself," she said gently.

"Indeed?" Witton asked quietly, not troubling to conceal the doubt in his voice. "And yet he has succeeded in causing you distress. In convincing you that you are not altogether the perfect image of a woman."

"You are refining too much upon what I said yesterday," Calista answered earnestly.

Then, as Witton continued to regard her with open disbelief, Calista turned away from him and busied herself once more with her work.

For a long moment Witton was content to watch her. Then, moving to stand behind Calista, he asked gently, "Are you so certain that I am?"

Defiantly, Calista faced him and said, "Quite certain, thank you." As he still eyed her doubtfully, Calista gave a sigh of exasperation. "It only wants a little resolution to throw off such nonsense as George Trumble speaks. You caught me yesterday in a missish mood, but most of the time, I assure you, I care not a whit what he says."

"Forgive me," Witton said coldly. "I was mistaken it seems."

Yet again Calista turned her back on him to work and for some minutes there was virtual silence in the small room and Witton began to regret the impulse that had made him seek her out. Then, as though she spoke with an effort, Calista said hesitantly, "Your fiancée must be very grateful when you champion *her* cause."

Startled, it took Witton a moment to recollect the tale he had told. But then he entered into things with, his mother would have said, a distressing degree of levity.

"Terribly grateful," he agreed coolly.

"Is she . . . is she conventional?" Calista asked, a touch of wistfulness to her voice.

"Extremely," Witton said with an innocent air. Then, outrageously, he went on, "She would not think of going out without her maid or a groom. She is an expert needlewoman, excels in the use of watercolors, sings like an angel, and plays the pianoforte effortlessly."

If Calista's shoulders drooped at these words, Witton appeared not to notice. Indeed, a smile twitched about the corners of his mouth as he watched her work and waited, patiently, for her to speak next.

"She sounds quite perfect," Calista said at last. "I am surprised you can bear to be away from her side."

"Oh," Witton said airily, "there is no rush. She will be waiting for me whenever I can see her again."

Calista set down the jar she was holding with a distinct thump. "You appear very sure of yourself," she said, biting off the words.

An unholy glee filled Witton's eyes as he said, "Why should I not be? She has waited long enough already, what are a few more days, weeks, or months?"

"Everything, I should think," Calista said tartly. "Unless, of course, you do not care that she may come to her senses and decide that you are a heartless fellow and she would be better off without you."

"No, no, that will never happen," Witton said with a satisfied air.

"Indeed? And why not?" Calista asked, gripping the edge of her work table tightly. "Does she love you so very much? Do you love her?"

She turned to face him then, her eyes searching his, and Witton found he had no more taste for this game. Stepping forward he gripped her shoulders and started to speak. "Miss Standish, there is something I must tell you. About my fiancée. She—"

"She is the most jealous creature alive," came a sudden voice from behind them. "Hallo, John, I was wondering where you were."

With a sigh of exasperation, Witton let go of Calista's shoulders and turned to face his friend. "Hallo, Freddy," he said impatiently. "Go away, will you? I've something I wish to tell Miss Standish."

"So I see," Leverton said impishly. "But I've something to tell you, so you may as well resign yourself and come along with me. Whatever you wish to tell Miss Standish can surely wait. You don't mind, do you, ma'am?"

Feeling a trifle breathless, Calista turned back to her work table. "Of course not," she said over her shoulder. "I've work to do, anyway. As for your fiancée, Mr. Witton, I cannot see that anything you might say about her could be of the least interest to me."

Witton hesitated and almost reached out toward Calista. Leverton forestalled him, however, and literally dragged him out of the small building. There, Witton shook off his mood and said, grimly, "Very well, Freddy, what is it that is so dashed important for you to tell me?"

Leverton merely took his friend by the arm and started off toward the woods that began near the side of the house. "Come take a walk," was all he would say until they were well out of earshot of the outbuildings.

At last, however, Witton was out of patience. "What the devil is going on?" he demanded, planting his feet firmly in the middle of the path.

"I am trying," Leverton retorted, "to save you from your own folly. What the devil did you think you were doing back there?"

"What do you mean?" Witton asked warily.

"I mean, taking Miss Standish by the shoulders and looking as if you were about to kiss her. By an open doorway, no less!" Leverton said in exasperation. "How long will anyone believe your tale of an attachment to someone else if you continue to behave like that?"

For a long moment Witton did not answer. At last he said quietly, "Had you not come in then, Freddy, I was about to tell Miss Standish that it was all a hoax anyway."

"Have you gone mad?" Leverton demanded incredulously. "You're the one who demanded we tell such a tale in the first place. You're the one who was so afraid of being pounced upon by a family eager to see Miss Standish married off to the first possible candidate."

"I begin to think that might not be such a terrible fate," Witton replied coolly.

Leverton gave a snort of disgust. "Yes, but do you want that to be your decision or theirs? How long do you think you would escape their web once they knew you liked Miss Standish and were unattached?" Freddy paused, then changed tactics. Coaxingly he said, "Talk with her. Get to know her. Stay on after I have gone, by all means. But give yourself the out of an attachment to someone else. Suppose after a week or so you discover you cannot abide the girl? What then?"

John Witton sighed heavily. "I cannot like such deceit," he said.

"That does you credit," Leverton said immediately. "But as the lies have already been spoken, why disillusion the family—distress them, if you will—unless you are certain you must? If, in time, you decide you like Miss Standish enough to marry her, then you may say the attachment is broken off and no one need be hurt. As they will be if you suddenly, blatantly, announce that you have been lying to them."

"Perhaps you are right," Witton said at last. "But I still do not like it."

"Of course I am right," Leverton retorted, clapping his friend on the shoulder. "And of course you don't like it. But I assure you that you would do well to be guided by me on the matter. You may be a Witton, accustomed to having your way about everything, but I have far more experience with the ladies. Trust me, I know what I am about. Now, as to why I went looking for you in the first place. You know, John, that I mean to go home tomorrow and I wanted to talk over with you certain matters still to be looked into. It is not fair, I know, to ask you to deal with them instead of me, but I am uneasy about Eleanor and want to return to her. Besides, you've a better head for figures than I do anyway."

This time Witton clapped his friend on the shoulder. "Go, then, Freddy," he said roughly. "And don't worry about the Standishes' affairs. Just tell me what I am to deal with and what may safely be left in other hands."

So, deep in conversation, they returned to the house. As for Calista, she found a number of tasks that kept her away from everyone for the rest of the day.

7

THE NEXT MORNING, Frederick Leverton courteously took his leave of the Standish household. It was, moreover, a simple matter to arrange that Witton stay on a while longer in his stead. Particularly as George Trumble had by then recollected just who John Witton was and taken Mrs. Standish and her daughters aside to tell them.

"To be sure, he hasn't a title," Trumble had said irritably, "but only the greenest flat could fail to recognize how high he stands in the *ton*. Yes, Mrs. Standish, he is one of *those* Wittons, with a fortune anyone might envy. I've heard it said he has forty thousand pounds a year and doesn't contrive to spend the half of it!"

"Is he, is he clutchfisted?" Mrs. Standish had asked a trifle anxiously.

"Not that I have heard," Trumble retorted shortly. "Nor, what's more important, likely to gamble it away like so many of his fellows."

"He sounds like a slow top to me!" Xanthe had said scornfully.

"That only shows how little you know,"

Trumble told her severely. "John Witton has the enviable reputation of a man who can drive a curricle superbly, hold his liquor well, cup a wafer with the best of them at Manton's, and possesses a keen skill at cards. If he has any lack, it is held to be a habit of frankness with the ladies. In any event, madam," Trumble had concluded, "he is the sort of gentleman any mother should be pleased to have take an interest in her daughters. For all his talk of an attachment, I have not heard it spoken about. That means it may yet be broken off. And," he had said, turning to Calista, "if you contrive to whistle down the wind a parti as eligible as this, who has apparently taken an interest in you, it will be a great deal too bad!"

Well, that had certainly given Amabel Standish a great deal to think about, and she was all affability when Leverton was ready to leave. Indeed, she insisted upon escorting him out to his carriage herself.

"I ought to stay myself, but with my wife having just had a baby . . ." Leverton allowed his voice to trail off.

Mrs. Standish nodded emphatically. "You wish to be with her. Quite right, and quite commendable too. Far better than this absurd notion some men seem to have that once they've had the pleasure of conceiving a child none of the rest of it should fall to them. Their wives are on their own with the business of birthing and raising and tending to the child. Besides, Oliver never should have imposed upon you in the first place. But he did. There it is and can't be changed. As for Mr. Witton, we shall be delighted to have him stay and shall do our best to make him feel at home here. It should not be much longer before he has everything settled, I am sure."

But it was. Somehow, necessary documents seemed to disappear overnight and not reappear for days. Or someone Witton needed to speak to could not be found. Inevitably, he spent a great deal of time in Calista's company, a circumstance that both found strangely agreeable. But Witton found that he enjoyed just as much the lively discussions that took place whenever two or more of the younger Standishes were together. They were remarkably well informed on many topics without having lost a naiveté that Witton found refreshing after the jaded tastes of London.

Whether it was comparing the theories of Stukeley and Aubrey over the stone circles to be found at Avebury, Stonehenge, and a great many other places in England, Scotland, and Wales, or discussing what ought to be done about India, Witton could scarcely claim to be bored. And as he watched Calista, he became increasingly convinced of her good sense and kind nature. Nor could he regret the fine training that allowed her to put her mind to far better use than most men he knew. Only George Trumble continued to be a thorn in his side, and Calista's, with his clumsy attempts to promote a match between the pair.

And Witton could not help but notice that under her brother-in-law's baleful eye she was prone to a constraint that did not occur otherwise. But as Trumble spent much of his time at the local pubs, even that proved no great obstacle.

The easy affection that had sprung up at once between John Witton and the members of the Standish family grew over the days that followed and he was soon treated as though he were one of the family.

Witton felt no surprise, therefore, a week later when Mrs. Standish spoke up over breakfast and said, "I don't like to impose upon you, Mr. Witton, but would you be able to take Calista to the fair near Corsham today? We need to hire some workers and Calista knows what is required. I had meant to go myself, but something has come up here."

"Certainly," Mr. Witton said easily. A trifle puzzled, however, he asked, "But surely it is a job better entrusted to Gilby?"

Mrs. Standish laughed. "We are in need of a kitchen girl and a laundry woman. I am afraid Gilby wouldn't have the slightest notion what to look for."

"Nor should I," Mr. Witton replied promptly.

"But you won't have to," Mrs. Standish said, wide-eyed. "I have already told you that Calista knows precisely how to go about the matter herself. I only ask you to go along because I cannot like the notion of her gallivanting about the countryside by herself. Gilby and Raynor are going, but they left before dawn because they were afraid they would miss some of the prize-fighting or the games or the menagerie the fair is rumored to possess. Heaven knows if Calista will even see them with all the crowds. Mr. Witton, there are sometimes some rather rough customers at these country fairs and I should like her to have someone with her in the event of trouble." She paused, then added frankly, "I could ask Mr. Trumble to go with Calista, but I should prefer it if you would."

"Of course I shall go with your daughter, Mrs. Standish. I should be delighted to do so," Witton answered honestly.

"Good. That's settled then," Mrs. Standish said, beaming with satisfaction. She turned to Calista, who had remained silent through this entire discussion. "You must be sure to tell the women they are required a week from today and give them explicit directions to our estate. Of course, if they wish to come sooner that is perfectly all right, but they must arrive during daylight."

"Yes, Mama," Calista said dutifully.

"And don't offer them a penny more than we agreed upon," her mother continued. "They shall try to take advantage of you, young as you are, you know. Though with Mr. Witton at your side, I have much less fear of that."

"Yes, Mama."

"Good. Then as soon as breakfast is over you had best be on your way."

"Yes, Mama."

Later, as they were driving in Witton's curricle to the fair, his curiosity got the better of him and he asked conversationally, "Suppose no one wishes to work for you at the wages you are willing to pay? Are you allowed to raise your offer then? Your mother does not appear to have thought of that possibility."

Calista laughed a full-throated laugh and Witton found himself thinking how delightful she was when she was not trying to fulfill her mother's notions of how a young lady ought to behave. So intent was he upon these thoughts that he almost missed what she had to say. "No fear of that, Mr. Witton," Calista said with a shake of her head that sent the curls dancing about the edges of her gray bonnet. "Everyone knows we pay the most generous wages hereabouts. As a result, there are always more than enough servants and farmhands willing to come work for us. One of Papa's more radical notions and one of the more successful ones. Even Mama finally had to agree that it was far pleasanter to have contented servants in the house than a few more pounds in the bank. Now she is as generous as Papa ever was."

Witton shook his head. "Now I have it," he told her playfully, "you are a family of spendthrifts. I am shocked to the depths of my soul!"

Calista laughed. "Nothing of the sort," she retorted, entering into the spirit of things. "Why think of how much we save in butcher and linen

and draper bills by never having a cook who spoils
the roast out of anger, or a laundry girl who
forgets and accidently ruins the sheets or a dress
or shirt or something. *Our* servants are much too
eager to keep their places to risk being careless."

"Aha, but you have lost two servants and must
search for new ones today," Witton said triumphantly. "Explain that one if you can!"

Primly Calista smoothed her skirts before she
answered. "Another of Papa's innovations. He
never discouraged the servants from courting.
Properly, of course. And even that works to our
advantage. No girl looking for her first post need
fear a future limited to drudgery. She knows that
with us she may still hope to marry and have a
home and children of her own someday. Not a few
become tenants on our land and help out when
needed at the house, from time to time. But we
have been short-handed for some time in the
laundry, and now the kitchen girl is leaving to
marry a young man who plans to work in
Chippenham and that is too far for her to come."

"Heavens, I had no notion your father was such
a radical!" Witton said, keeping a neat hand on the
reins.

"Only in some ways, I assure you," Calista
replied with a wry smile. "And only when it suited
him. Were he still alive he would have been off
with Gilby and Raynor at dawn to see the
curiosities at the fair, just as eager as they are.
But it would not occur to him to give the servants
the entire day off to do so as well."

Witton laughed. "In that your father was scarcely unique," he said. "My father would have been just the same, I assure you!"

Curious, Calista asked, "What was, or should I say is, your father like?"

"My father died some years ago," he said quietly, "and I have not ceased to miss him. So much so that I rarely spend time at my own estate, a circumstance my mother has long complained of. My father also liked books and learning and dreamed of seeing other countries, though his health did not allow of much traveling. He was used to say that he hoped I would someday see the places he could only read about." Witton paused, then added, "He would have liked your family. It is a great pity he never knew your father. But come, tell me about the fair. What must I expect? Bull baiting? Sheep? Cattle? A hiring corner, that much I know for certain."

"Sheep and cattle and the hiring fair," Calista agreed, a twinkle in her eyes, "thought I am not sure about the bull. Some horses, though not many, I fear, and none to match these chestnuts of yours. Prizefighting, games, perhaps a menagerie, Mama already mentioned those. Let me see, what might interest you? Gypsies? There are sure to be some of those. Perhaps a roundabout, and last year Gilby was most impressed with the smoking oyster."

"The what?" Witton asked incredulously.

"The smoking oyster," Calista replied innocently. Carefully she avoided meeting his eyes as she smoothed her skirt and said, "Myself, I thought they must have used a dead oyster and had a small boy under the table Gilby said it rested upon, blowing the smoke, but Gilby swore it was all real. Of course, as he also came home with his pocket picked and only a handful of coins left, which turned out not to be genuine, I do not set great store in his opinion."

Witton laughed. "How much he sounds like me at my first fair," he said. "Though I was wiser. I had my fortune told and was promised great things in my future. I was to travel, become a hero of sorts, come into great wealth, and marry late but sire twelve children."

"How . . . how encouraging," Calista said faintly.

"Yes, wasn't it?" Witton said with relish. "I thought so. Until, at any rate, I compared my fortune with my friend Leverton's. Exactly the same one except that he was to have only seven children instead of twelve, a circumstance I felt tilted matters heavily in his favor."

Witton ended on so mournful a note that Calista could not help but laugh. "After such a daunting fortune I am surprised you do not avoid fairs like the plague," she said.

"Ah, but you see I am doomed to attend them, seeking to have my fortune told at each, hoping someone will give me a better one," Witton retorted, a distinct twinkle in his eyes.

"And do they?" Calista asked obligingly.

Mournfully Witton shook his head. "Sometimes I get wealth, sometimes health, and more than once the promise I would be a hero. But for the rest, everyone tells me I am to father twelve children, a circumstance I find, as you say, most daunting!"

"Well," Calista said decisively, her own eyes dancing merrily, "now I understand the reason for your fiancée's patience. She must find the notion of mothering twelve children more than a little daunting herself! Indeed, I am astonished that it was not enough to make you swear off marriage."

Witton turned to Calista with an approving smile. "Now that is just what I would have done if I could. How clever of you to hit upon the precise solution so quickly. I confess that it took me some years to do so. Unfortunately, matchmaking mamas, my own included, refused to believe me when I told them so. Even my fiancée thinks I am joking when I talk this way."

Calista replied in mock astonishment, "Do they indeed? I cannot credit it! How could they think you had too much sense to believe in fortune tellers?"

With wide eyes Witton regarded Calista. "Why, Miss Standish," he said reprovingly, "surely you believe in fortune tellers? Or, at least, have an open mind upon the matter? Your father must have taught you never to dismiss anything out of hand."

Once more there was a martial glint in Calista's eye as she said, "Sir, you are trying to gammon me and I do not take kindly to the attempt."

Witton's shoulders shook with suppressed

laughter but he contented himself with shaking his head and saying mournfully, "I see you do not believe me either. How lowering."

Calista merely chuckled and they reached the fair in the best of spirits. Once there, acquaintances, particularly ladies, might have been astonished to see the easy way Witton laughed and talked with Miss Standish and the gallant way he sheltered her from the press of the crowds. Or the enthusiastic way he entered into the entertainments offered at the fair after Miss Standish had concluded her business at the hiring square.

Of course, they encountered Gilby and Raynor at the Collection of Living Curiosities, since it seemed Gilby was viewing the creatures for the seventh time that day. "I am sure there is some fakery about the mermaid," he told Calista and Witton, "I have just not yet figured out how it is done."

Kindly, Witton and Calista suppressed their laughter and left the brothers staring at the tank in which she sat. As they started to walk away, Gilby called out, "When do you mean to go back home, Cal?"

"We're not yet certain," Witton replied for her. "Why? Did you wish to go back with us?"

Gilby shrugged and said, "Dunno," while Raynor looked on, embarrassed.

"Well if you do," Witton said kindly, "I have driven my curricle and you will find it near the stand of oaks."

"Thank you, sir," Raynor said hastily, with a frown at his brother, "but I expect we'll want to stay later than you will. There's some, er, dancing and such."

Thinking to himself that he understood very well, that the boys were unlikely to come to any real harm, and that, in any event, it really wasn't his affair, Witton nodded to Gilby and said, easily, "Right. Well, if you change your mind, you know where to find my curricle. And if you don't, I shall understand perfectly."

As they walked away Witton could hear Raynor's exasperated voice asking his brother, "Now what the devil did you mean by all of that, Gil? Why on earth would we want to go back with them?"

Outside the menagerie, Witton and Calista stopped at several booths, where he tried his hand at some games. Again the ladies of London would have been astonished to see the pride and gallantry with which he presented one thimble and two combs to Miss Standish and the gentle way he adjusted the locket about her neck when the ribbon came undone.

Calista could not entirely repress a shiver as his fingers touched the back of her neck. "Are you cold?" Witton asked at once, the concern evident in his voice.

Hastily, Calista shook her head, grateful that the rim of her bonnet hid her face as she said, untruthfully, "No. Yes. A little." Turning, she looked up at Witton as she said, a trifle wistfully,

"Perhaps it is time we were returning home. The sky is turning dark and I'm afraid it might rain."

"You're right, we should go," Witton said with alacrity. "Though I very much fear that we may not make it back before the storm breaks. Still, the closer we are, the better."

Calista hesitated only a moment before she said, "There is a way we might make it. The road is not so good as the one by which we came, but it is shorter."

Curtly, Witton nodded and replied, "By all means let us take the shorter route. Let's go. Or should we look for your brothers and warn them as well?"

Decisively, Calista shook her head. "They wouldn't listen anyway and we haven't the time to try to find them. The grounds are more crowded than ever."

With another nod, Witton took Calista's arm and guided her through the crowd, moving with surprising speed.

8

Both Witton and Calista were unusually silent as they traveled back toward the Standish estate. Calista confined her comments to directions as to the turns Witton should take. He confined himself to confirming her directions and asking occasionally how far they still had to go. The greater part of his attention was fixed on the road ahead, which was, Calista confessed, in worse order than she had remembered. They were still some distance from their destination when the first raindrops began to fall. Within minutes they were both soaked to the skin and when it seemed nothing further could go wrong, the curricle hit something in the road and an axle gave way. Witton struggled to control the horses as Calista was thrown against him.

When he had succeeded and the chestnuts had been brought to a standstill, Witton climbed down and surveyed the damage, still holding tight to the reins. Seeing the grim expression in his eyes, Calista climbed down after him.

Taking a deep breath, she said, "We shall have

to ride the horses home and send out someone to repair this tomorrow."

Curtly, Witton nodded. "The horses are not accustomed to the saddle, of course, but then we haven't any saddles anyway. How will you manage?" he asked Calista.

She looked down at her narrow-skirted walking dress that was already ruined by the rain. An experienced horsewoman, she knew she could not ride to the side and hope to stay on the creature's slippery back in the rain. "I shall have to tear my skirt and ride astride," she said quietly. "I see nothing else for it."

Grimly, Witton nodded. "The alternative is to leave you here on your own, and that I cannot prefer. But will your mother forgive the lapse in propriety, do you think?"

"She must," Calista retorted tartly, "for I do not intend to catch my death of cold to satisfy anyone."

"Good," Witton said, turning to unhitch the horses from their traces.

He had scarcely done so, however, when lightning flashed overhead, frightening the horses. Even his strong hands were not able to hold them as they bolted and Witton and Calista were left with the discouraging sight of the two chestnuts racing down the road in the rain.

More grimly than ever, Witton turned to Calista and said, "Now what do we do? How far is it to walk?"

The quaver in her voice betrayed how tired and discouraged Calista felt as she replied, "Above three miles, I'm afraid. And the road will rapidly be growing muddy. Nor, with the lightning, will it be safe. Perhaps we should seek shelter at a farmhouse or even in a barn in a pinch. Somewhere, for a little while. The storm may blow over and then we could try for home. There are some farms hereabouts, I know."

Witton nodded and swiftly scanned the horizon looking for a light or at least the outline of a building against the sky. After a moment he pointed and said, "Over there. I think I see something."

"Anything is better than standing in this rain," Calista agreed promptly.

Pausing only to retrieve the lantern and blanket he kept beneath the seat of his curricle, Witton led the way at a steady pace for the structure he had seen. Calista followed without complaint, indeed passing ahead of him as soon as she saw where they were headed.

Never had a field seemed so huge before, but soon enough they had reached the door of what appeared to be some sort of outbuilding. It was evident the thing had been some time abandoned and that the roof leaked and the wind whistled through the walls. But it was far dryer than outside and Witton and Calista gratefully entered.

Witton lost no time in lighting the lantern while Calista shivered under the blanket he had thrown about her shoulders. Seeing her distress he said, "I would light a fire but I am afraid the whole building would go up in flames if I did."

Calista managed a wan smile as she shook her head and said, "I shall be fine. Indeed, Gilby and Raynor will quite envy me when they hear what an adventure I have had."

Moving to her side Witton looked down at Calista and said, admiringly, "What an extraordinary young woman you are, Miss Standish."

In spite of herself Calista laughed. "Why? Because I do not scream or faint or otherwise give way to the megrims? Pray tell me what that would accomplish," she said tartly.

"Nevertheless, most of your sex would," Witton countered.

Abruptly, Calista turned away. Over her shoulder she said, "I am well aware that I lack many maidenly virtues, Mr. Witton. You need not remind me."

All caution forgotten, Witton placed his hands on her shoulders and his voice was warm as he replied, "Never say so, Miss Standish. I meant it not as a complaint, but rather a compliment. You are delightful just as you are."

And then, the light from the lantern flickering on her face, Calista turned around and looked up at Witton wonderingly. With a hiss of astonishment he realized that there was nothing he wanted more than to take her in his arms and make love to her. "I—" he began, then broke off knowing there was nothing he wanted to say that he dared say.

Unaware that she was doing so, Calista lifted up a hand as though to touch his cheek. In a shaky voice she said, "I think it is you who are extraordinary, Mr. Witton. Any other gentleman I know would be complaining about his drenched clothing or bolted horses or muddy boots. I think it most kind of you not to rail at me for the predicament in which we now find ourselves."

As she spoke, Witton had caught Calista's hand in his and raised it to his lips. With a rallying smile he said, "Ah, but then I have never aspired to the dandy set, Miss Standish, and I consider it a calumny that you think I might. Besides, as you said before, what would a fit of temper accomplish now?"

Calista shivered at the touch of his hand upon hers and at once Witton was all concern. "Come, you must sit down," he said. "You are no doubt tired and hungry and cold, for I roundly confess I am all three."

"And wet," Calista managed to add as she allowed him to guide her to a pile of old straw that at least had the advantage of being dry.

Carefully, Witton settled the blanket more firmly about her shoulders but Calista could not help but see that he, too, was shivering with the cold. Without a word, as he sat down beside her, Calista lifted part of the blanket and placed it around his shoulders as well so that they sat side by side sharing its limited warmth.

Conscious of how close they were to one another, Calista tried to think of something to say. At last she said, "This cannot be what you are accustomed to, Mr. Witton."

"Nor you, I should think," he replied gravely, looking with concern at her pale face.

To his surprise, Calista laughed. "On the contrary," she replied after a moment. "Not that I am accustomed, precisely, but more than once when Papa took me on a botanical expedition to gather various plants hereabouts he managed to get lost just when a storm was coming on. I assure you I have taken shelter in a barn before."

"But not," Witton said in the same grave voice as before, "with a stranger."

Abruptly, Calista sobered. "No, not with a stranger," she agreed in a low voice. "Though after the past week you no longer seem such a stranger to me."

Still Witton persisted. "I think we may find ourselves in the devil of a pickle if the rain does not let up tonight," he said quietly. "I cannot think it likely anyone will find us before morning. Your mother will be most concerned."

"She—she will know I must have taken shelter somewhere," Calista said with constraint. "There is no need for her to know it was not alone."

Witton shook his head but, seeing her distress, forebore to press Calista further. Time enough in the morning for that, he thought. Instead, he strove to distract her with one amusing story after another. Overhead the roof still dripped rain from the storm and the sound of crashing thunder attested to its continuing violence. Eventually, some hours later, as the rain steadily drummed on the roof, Witton and Calista slept.

When the storm began, Amabel Standish did not at once begin to worry. She was accustomed to her sons taking shelter wherever they were on such occasions and Calista was, after all, in the capable care of Mr. Witton. Calmly she gave orders to the kitchen that only four covers should be set for supper but that they should be prepared to serve trays to the others whenever they straggled in.

George Trumble, of course, had a number of disapproving things to say over dinner about young people who gave no thought to time, but Mrs. Standish merely observed that she hoped her children were enjoying themselves; and that she would not ever wish to keep them too closely hedged about.

It was only after she had seen Xanthe tucked in for the night and the thunder long since ended that she began to wonder where her children were. To be sure, the rain drummed steadily on the roof, but that should not have stopped them from returning. Still, it was only wonder she felt and not concern. It was left to George to express these thoughts aloud, but even Amethyst was finally moved to tell him shortly, "Don't be such a doom-sayer, George! My brothers and sister are well able to take care of themselves, I assure you. Mama and Papa have always allowed us a great deal of freedom."

By ten o'clock, however, wonder had given way to concern, and when Gilby and Raynor walked in, alone, at eleven o'clock, Amabel Standish felt distinctly alarmed.

"Been gone a devilish long time, haven't you?" Mr. Trumble said reprovingly.

"Where are Calista and Mr. Witton?" Mrs. Standish asked, ignoring her son-in-law.

Gilby and Raynor looked at one another, then at their mother. "Dunno," Raynor said. "Aren't they back yet? They left hours before we did."

"Well, they have not yet returned," Mr. Trumble said heavily. "I am surprised you did not pass them on the road."

"We didn't see them as we came back along the main route," Gilby said thoughtfully. "P'rhaps they tried a shortcut."

"Not in the rain, surely," Raynor snorted. "Cal would know better than that!"

"Yes, but what if they left before the rain started?" Gilby persisted.

Begrudgingly, Raynor nodded. "Wouldn't be surprised if they came a cropper then. Probably had to take shelter at one of the farmhouses if they did. Should we go and look for them, do you think?" he asked his mother.

"In those wet things?" Mrs. Standish demanded, clucking over both boys.

"Besides," Gilby added dryly, "I expect it will start thundering and lightning again very soon and I shouldn't care to be outside when it does. You know what Papa told us about the experiments by that American, Mr. Franklin."

Slowly Raynor nodded. Then, with a shrug, he said, "Cal can take care of herself and Mr. Witton is with her so they'll be all right. But I shall roast her when we see her over the folly of taking that road!"

"Roast her?" Trumble said, thunderstruck. "As though the matter were as casual as that. My dear Mrs. Standish, surely you must see that matters are serious indeed?"

Hastily, Mrs. Standish told her sons, "Go and change into dry things. I'll ring for Mary to bring trays for you to eat in here as soon as you have done so. All right?"

"Perfect, Mama," Raynor said, kissing her on the cheek.

With a devilish gleam in his eye Gilby added, "Don't worry about Cal, Mama. After all, she is your daughter."

With a shooing motion, Amabel Standish sent her sons upstairs and rang for the maid. George Trumble was still not satisfied. "Upon my words, Mrs. Standish, you are taking this mighty calmly," he said. "Surely you mean to do something more to look for them?" he demanded.

Mrs. Standish, who felt her own patience had been tried sorely enough, said bluntly, "Since we have no notion where Calista and Mr. Witton may be, not even for certain what road they took, I do not see that there is anything we can do. Unless, sir, you are offering your services to go out into the rain to look for them."

At this Trumble blanched and, correctly taking this to mean he was not, she went on, a trifle more gently, "Really, Mr. Trumble, I do share some of your concern. But for all we know, they put up at some snug inn or farmhouse and are perfectly all right. In any event, I do not see what can be done before morning, for I will not send my poor boys out again in the rain."

And it was true, Mrs. Standish reflected to herself, that the farmers hereabouts all knew the Standishes and they would see that Calista came to no harm. Not one would refuse her shelter— indeed, they were likely to insist upon offering it.

Grumbling, Trumble said shortly, "Well, madam, if you are satisfied, I suppose it is not for me to cavil. Good night. Are you coming, Amethyst?"

Throwing an apologetic look to her mother, Amethyst rose to her feet and said, meekly enough, "Yes, George."

Gratefully, Mrs. Standish watched them go upstairs.

9

IT WAS JUST after breakfast the next morning when the knocker sounded at the front door. Amabel Standish happened to be crossing through the foyer and therefore was treated to the sight of her daughter's and Witton's return. Straw protruded from Witton's rumpled clothes and hair, though it was evident he had made a rudimentary attempt to wash himself up. Calista was worse. Not only did the straw protrude from her hair and clothes, her bonnet was crushed beyond recognition and with horror Mrs. Standish realized her dress was torn at the hem.

Following her mother's mortified gaze, Calista looked down at her dress, then said, ruefully, "I thought I was going to have to ride astride and had just begun to tear it when the horses bolted."

Too stunned to reply, Mrs. Standish could only stare at the pair while the servant who had opened the door struggled manfully not to do so. As they stood there, Gilby, Raynor, and Xanthe all came running down the stairs, while at the sound of the clatter, Amethyst and Mr. Trumble emerged from the parlor. "Mama," Raynor called out, "Xanthe said she saw farmer Darby's cart from her window driving away. Did he bring word of—"

Raynor broke off at the sight of Calista and Witton. Behind him, Gilby and Xanthe came to an abrupt halt as well.

"Good God!" Trumble expostulated.

With commendable composure Mrs. Standish roused herself to say, "I think we had best all go into the drawing room and Mr. Witton and Calista can tell us of their adventure."

Politely, Witton said, "May we change our clothes, first, Mrs. Standish?"

Flustered, she replied hastily, "Oh, my, yes, of course. I shall have the servants bring up hot water at once."

Witton bowed and headed up the stairs, not waiting for the rest of what Mrs. Standish might have to say. A trifle more slowly, Calista followed.

Only her acute awareness of the interested gaze of the servants prevented Mrs. Standish from immediately joining her daughter. Instead, she gave the orders for bath water to be taken upstairs, then forced herself to smile and say to her other children, "Come, we shall wait for them in the drawing room."

Demurely, Gilby, Raynor, and Xanthe went with their mother. But they broke into loud discussion of what had occurred the moment they were behind closed doors. As for George Trumble, he seated himself beside her and said, "My dear Mrs.

Standish, I feel for you. Someone must bring Mr. Witton to book for this. As I know that you have no man to act for you, may I offer my services?"

Amethyst tugged at her husband's arm, saying, "But George, we don't even know yet what occurred!"

"But Amethyst, my dear . . ."

Mrs. Standish did not answer or try to stop anyone from talking but just sat in her corner of the room, eyes closed, while she waited for Calista and Witton to come back downstairs. Somehow, she was not at all eager to hear the entire story, she thought to herself.

Upstairs, Calista nervously, hastily, bathed and dressed, scarcely aware of what she was putting on.

John Witton, acutely aware of the consequences of what had occurred, took greater care. He should, he supposed, have been more distressed. Certainly his valet was appalled by the state of affairs.

"Your suit, sir, utterly ruined," the valet said plaintively as he helped Witton remove the offending garment. "And I don't know if I shall ever be able to make your boots shine as they ought to."

"If need be I can replace them, Jeffries," Witton replied calmly.

"Yes, but the rest won't be so easy, mark my words," Jeffries said darkly. "Not according to what I've been hearing, anyways."

Witton paused in the act of stepping into the hip bath. "And what have you been hearing?" he asked with a frown.

Handing his employer the soap, Jeffries answered expressionlessly, "That you was out all night, sir, *with* the young lady of the house. That the family tried to put it about that you was caught in the rain and took shelter with some farm family or other. But the servants wasn't buying it. Said you was a no-good fellow from London what had got the young lady into trouble and ought to be made to do right by her."

"I see," Witton said, regarding his valet with great interest. "And what did you say to all this?"

His face still devoid of expression, Jeffries replied, "I told them, sir, that you were not the sort nor never would be to compromise a young lady. And that if they didn't stop saying so I would forget that it was beneath my dignity to notice them and draw the cork from more than a few of their noses."

In spite of himself, Witton laughed. "Good man," he said.

"Yes, but what will happen?" Jeffries asked gloomily. "I don't suppose you was with a farmer's family overnight?"

Witton sighed. "No, I was not. Miss Standish and I were stranded, alone, in a cursed barn somewhere." He paused, then added, just before putting his head under the water to rinse it, "I suppose I shall have to marry the girl."

When he came up out of the water, Witton found Jeffries sputtering helplessly. "Marry her?" the valet asked, his voice a trifle shrill. "Whatever can you mean, sir?"

"I thought my words were clear, Jeffries," Witton said innocently.

Jeffries swallowed. "Yes, sir, they were. But, sir, if nothing happened. . . . I mean, it's positively medieval, sir, to marry the girl just because you was caught overnight."

"Her family won't think so," Witton countered. Jeffries sputtered helplessly again and, as he heaved himself out of the tub, Witton took pity on his man. "Peace, Jeffries. I don't mean to see myself forced into anything. If I marry Miss Standish, it will be because I wish to, not because I have to. Though I would not harm the girl for the world. To be sure, it is all happening a trifle faster than I had intended, but I think it would have come to this in the end anyway."

With his jaw hanging open, Jeffries stared at his employer. Finally, Witton asked for his clean clothes and the valet hastened to hand them over. "Never say, sir, that you've fallen in love with the girl," he managed to say at last.

"Why not?" Witton asked with a frown. "Do you find her such an antidote?"

"Of . . . of course not, sir," Jeffries said hastily. "It's just that I've never . . . that is I'd begun to think you wouldn't . . . that is—"

"That is quite enough," Witton said with an

amused smile. "As for what you are trying to say, that you thought I would never fall prey to cupid's arrows, it seems you were mistaken. Much to my own surprise I find I am, indeed, in love with Miss Standish. And I don't even know yet if Miss Standish will have me."

"She will," Jeffries said to himself with absolute certainty. "She will."

When he emerged from his room Witton found Calista in the hallway, twisting her hands nervously together. His brows drew together in a frown of concern as he said, "Were you waiting for me?"

Reluctantly, Calista nodded. "It is no doubt foolish of me," she said, "but I did not wish to face Mama alone."

At the sight of her distress Witton found himself wanting very much to comfort her. With a reassuring smile he said, "Come, let us beard the lion together then."

Gratefully, Calista took his arm. At the foot of the stairs, Calista stepped away from Witton and, taking a deep breath, opened the door to the drawing room. As always, Witton found himself thinking that it was a pretentious name for the small, cluttered room, but he did not say so. Instead, he bowed to Mrs. Standish, who rose at their entrance.

"Come in, Calista, Mr. Witton," she said with creditable calm. "I have arranged for some tea, and it has already arrived. I thought you might like some after your, er, adventure."

"Yes, what happened?" Xanthe broke in eagerly. "Gil and Ray said you left the fair even before they did and *they* got home last night!"

George Trumble came to stand beside Witton and said with a cough, "Perhaps you and I should speak privately, sir."

"I don't think so," Witton told him shortly. Then, ignoring Xanthe as well, he said to Mrs. Standish, "I should like some tea, thank you, Mrs. Standish."

"I'll pour it," Calista said hastily.

"Mr. Witton—" Trumble said, more sternly.

"George, do sit down. This is my household and I thank you for your concern but it is my duty to handle matters, not yours," Amabel Standish told her son-in-law tartly.

"Yes, but what happened, Calista?" Xanthe persisted.

"Quiet!" Gilby told her under his breath. "She'll tell us when she's ready."

Xanthe ignored her brother. "Did you stay with the Darbys last night?" she asked. "What happened to your curricle? And your horses? I saw you come back in Darby's cart. Wasn't that uncomfortable?"

"*Xanthe!*" Mrs. Standish said reprovingly from between gritted teeth.

George Trumble glowered from the sofa on which he had seated himself and Amethyst patted his arm comfortingly.

Witton took the tea Calista offered him with a quiet "Thank you," then said to Mrs. Standish,

"It's all right. The child is only asking the things you must all be wondering. I should like to be able to tell you that we stayed the night with the Darbys, but we did not. We were returning from the fair last night when my curricle broke an axle. The road was deserted and my horses bolted, frightened by the lightning. There was nothing for it but to take shelter in the nearest structure, which was a deserted barn or outbuilding of some sort. This morning Mr. Darby found us and kindly offered us a ride home in his cart."

"And brought us round to the front door, though I assure you we would have preferred to slip in unseen," Calista added dryly.

Witton nodded, then went on. "Somehow I shall have to arrange for my curricle to be repaired and try to discover if anyone has seen my horses."

"You must have taken the shortcut then," Gilby said thoughtfully.

Witton nodded. "We did. It was evident a storm was coming on and the shortcut was our only hope of reaching here before it broke."

"So you spent the night alone together?" Xanthe said aloud in breathy wonder.

Witton met Mrs. Standish's eyes squarely as he said, "We did, ma'am. I suppose you will want us to post the banns."

That brought Calista to her feet. She had been sitting back, content to let Witton speak for both of them, but now she spoke, disbelief strong in her voice. "What? Are you mad? There isn't any reason to post banns—nothing happened last night!"

"Stap me if that isn't handsome of the fellow!" Trumble said from his seat.

As though he had not heard either of them, John Witton went on, "Or would a Special License be better, Mrs. Standish? And if so, do you know the closest place to obtain one?"

"From the bishop at Wells," she said at once. "Under the circumstances I think it might be better."

Calista looked from one to the other. "Better?" she demanded incredulously. "But what if I don't want to get married?"

Gilby snorted. As Calista looked at her brother, he said impatiently, "Oh, come, Cal, you're not a fool! You know dashed well that however innocently you spent your time, everyone will think the worst when they know you spent the night alone with Mr. Witton in a barn."

"But they need not know," Calista protested.

"Damme if the girl ain't mad," Trumble said roundly and encountered such a glare from Witton that he broke off hastily before saying more.

"Darby will not be able to resist spreading the tale," Mrs. Standish told her daughter evenly when the room was once more silent.

Calista turned to Witton. "Surely you cannot be serious," she said earnestly. "You know as well as I there is no reason for us to be married save for foolish gossip, which you need not regard for I most assuredly will not."

Witton looked down at Calista and took both her hands in his. "No, you would not regard it, would you?" he said with a smile. "But would it really be such a terrible fate to be married to me?" he asked coaxingly.

Calista could not meet his eyes and instead stared at the buttons of his coat as she said, "I— that is, of course not."

"Then why do you fight so hard against the notion?" he persisted.

"Because she's mad," Trumble repeated, but not so loudly this time that either could hear him.

Now Calista did look up into his eyes as she blurted out, "What about your fiancée?"

Witton hesitated, then replied, "There was no formal announcement. She will, I assure you, understand." Calista did not at once answer and he went on, rallyingly, "I see what it is, it's the twelve children you fear!"

"Twelve children?" Xanthe exclaimed.

"Mr. Witton, whatever do you mean?" Mrs. Standish demanded.

"P'rhaps he's as mad as she is," Trumble observed to no one in particular.

But both John Witton and Calista were oblivious to everyone else. With a gurgle of laughter she said, "You are absurd! But I will not marry anyone because someone says that I must."

"Very well then," Witton said quietly, raising

her hand to his lips. "Miss Calista Standish, will you marry me? Simply because you want to and I want to, and not because someone else says that we must?"

For perhaps the first time in a good many years, Calista acted without thinking the matter through. "Yes!" she said, a shy smile filling her own face.

There was a distinct sigh of relief from Mrs. Standish, while Raynor snorted in disgust and Xanthe said with a sigh, "How romantic."

"That's all right and tight, then," Trumble added with a satisfied air.

Witton turned to Mrs. Standish and said quietly, "If you will give me directions and lend me a horse, I shall ride over to see the bishop today."

"Of course," she said at once. Then, with a slightly malicious air she added, "Perhaps Mr. Trumble will go with you and show you the way."

George Trumble blanched, but then rose to the occasion. "Happy to be of service," he said.

"Must it be done so quickly?" Calista asked with some concern. "Won't that make people believe the worst?"

Once again Witton smiled reassuringly. "No I shall tell everyone that I did not wish to wait. And that because you were in mourning I married you out of hand. No one will be surprised, I promise you, that I did not consult your feelings on the matter."

"But your family," Calista persisted. "Will they not wish to be here?"

This time Witton hesitated. "My mother is not well enough to travel," he said after a moment, "and would not expect to be here. My father is dead. That leaves only my brother, Edwin. And various aunts and uncles and cousins whom you would not wish to be plagued with, I assure you."

"Nevertheless, it would be better, perhaps, if your mother and brother, at least, were invited and the wedding set for a week from now," Mrs. Standish said slowly. "One ought to give them the chance to come if they could."

Witton bowed. "As you wish. Nevertheless, I should like to call upon the bishop today, as soon as I have sent off the message to my mother. A week is not three, and we would not have time to post the banns."

Mrs. Standish nodded. "Of course. And as I said, Mr. Trumble shall go with you."

10

THE DAYS PASSED quickly. The horses were found, the curricle repaired, invitations sent, and Calista's bridal clothes procured. If the Standish family felt any qualms about the approaching marriage they did not say so to Witton. Indeed, it seemed to him that matters moved forward with astonishing haste. The Special License was easily obtained, and the local churchman enlisted to perform the ceremony in the chapel adjoining the Standish home.

"It dates from the fifteenth century and the Standishes have always been married there," said the vicar, Mr. Forster, as he and Witton sat in his study. "Some of the windows are the originals, I believe, as are the windbraces."

Mr. Witton leaned back in his chair, regarding Mr. Forster steadily. "How interesting," he said politely.

The vicar fiddled with some papers on his desk, cleared his throat, then said nervously, "You must be thinking it very odd of me to have asked you to come and see me."

"Not at all," Witton said as politely as before. "I collect you are a friend of the family and wonder at the sudden nature of my attachment to Miss Standish."

Mr. Forster cleared his throat. "To be quite frank with you, Mr. Witton, yes I do. And I believe that while I am a friend to the whole family, my attachment of long standing to Miss Calista gives me the right to take an interest in her wedding to you. Quite aside from my role as officiator at the ceremony."

Witton, whose expression had been one of cool interest, now sat up sharply as he said, "*Your* longstanding attachment to Miss Standish?"

Mr. Forster permitted himself a small smile. "Yes, mine. Does that surprise you? We clerics are quite human, I assure you."

"Does Miss Standish, er, return your sentiments?" Witton asked, leaning back in his chair again.

The vicar avoided Witton's eyes. Rising from his chair, he walked over to the window and stood there, hands clasped behind his back. With a heavy sigh he said, "I do not know how Miss Standish feels about my attachment to her. When I approached her father to ask permission to pay my addresses to her, he refused, point-blank. He said he did not like what I would turn her into."

"And what was that?" Witton asked, curious.

"A proper woman!" Mr. Forster replied with an explosive breath. "I can only deprecate the eccentricity that led Oliver Standish to raise his daughter in such an extraordinary way. I have told Miss Standish more than once that I do not consider science a proper occupation for a woman."

"And how did she, er, take these pronouncements of yours?" Witton asked, with a barely suppressed smile.

"Aye, you may laugh at me," Forster said severely, "but Miss Standish did not. She answered me, with becoming reserve, that it was for her parents to advise her."

"How did you reply to that?" Witton asked.

"I could not disagree, however strongly I might regret, as I have said, the eccentricity that would lead a father to so ill advise a daughter," Mr. Forster said grudgingly. "Still, I have believed and continue to believe that were she only to accept my hand in marriage, I could exert a beneficial influence upon Miss Standish."

"Indeed?" Witton asked skeptically. "And if you could not? If she persisted in pursuing her researches?"

"She could not," Forster replied heavily. "If persuasion had not worked I would have forbidden it outright."

"Forgive me," Witton said hesitantly, "but if you so disapprove of Miss Standish, why would you ever have wanted to marry her in the first place?"

Again Forster sighed. "You have seen her. You

wish to marry her. Indeed, you are going to marry her. How can you ask?"

"Nevertheless I do," Witton pointed out gently.

Forster sat down again and regarded Witton across the desk. "Her nature is amiable," he said quietly, "and her breeding excellent, in spite of her father's attempts to betray it. She has, moreover, a kind and gentle side that would well befit a vicar's wife. And her portion is acceptable."

"I see," Witton said thoughtfully.

"May I ask why you are marrying her?" Forster asked sharply. When Witton hesitated the vicar went on, "I have heard rumors, you see, and I wish to be certain that Miss Standish is not making an error in marrying you."

At this Witton was amused. "And if you thought she was, what could you do to stop us?" he asked.

"You are pleased to smile about it," Forster said severely. "I cannot like that in you. If I thought Miss Calista was marrying you because of something that occurred which she felt marred her chances for marriage, I should go to her at once and offer to marry her myself, in spite of her family's opposition to the match."

"Brave words," Witton said soberly. "And by all means do so, if you wish. But I think you will find that Miss Standish is marrying me for the same reason that I am marrying her: because we both believe we shall suit."

The vicar permitted himself a very unpleasant smile. "Indeed? How well Miss Standish hides her feelings, then. She once did me the honor of confiding to me the qualities she looked for, some-day, in a husband. I trust you will not be offended if I tell you that save for your fortune, you appear to possess none of them."

His own eyes sparkling dangerously, Witton rose to his feet. Forster did so as well. "I understand you tolerably well, I think, and appreciate your concern," Witton said curtly. "But I assure you that I shall do my best to make Miss Standish happy. And if she does not think I am capable of doing so, it is for her to tell me herself!"

With the same unpleasant smile upon his face, the vicar said smoothly, "I only trust she will do so before it is too late."

"That is, if you are right," Witton said grimly.

Mr. Forster merely bowed.

"Good day, Mr. Forster, I shall see you on my wedding day," Witton said, a distinct snap in his voice.

"Good day, Mr. Witton," the vicar said, with the same unpleasant smile as before.

Once outside the vicarage, Witton took a deep breath and, setting off in the direction of the Standish household, scolded himself roundly. "The fellow is a jackanapes. Doubtless jealous because Calista will have you and not him. You are a fool to pay the slightest attention to anything he may have to say."

Witton might have succeeded in convincing himself of that if he had not encountered Calista coming back from the village before him, basket in hand.

"Miss Standish," he called.

She stopped and turned around, smiling shyly at the sight of him. It was the first time they had been alone together since the fair, for however eager her family might be for the wedding, Mrs. Standish was adamant that no further ammunition for gossip should present itself to the servants or anyone else.

"Hello, Mr. Witton," Calista said, waiting until he caught up with her.

In spite of himself, Witton smiled. "We are very formal with one another, aren't we," he said wryly. "Perhaps you had better call me John and I shall call you Calista, if I may."

"Of course."

They walked in silence for a few moments, then Witton cleared his throat and said, "I have just come from the vicarage."

"Oh?" Calista said doubtfully.

"Yes, I have seen Mr. Forster. He seems to have a high regard for you," Witton said gravely.

Calista looked up at her fiancé and said, a trifle earnestly, "Mr. Forster has a high regard for someone he thinks I could be."

"He believes that you might return his affection were it not for your maidenly modesty. Is he correct?" Witton asked quietly.

Calista laughed and a dimple appeared in her cheek as she replied, "On the contrary, it is my maidenly modesty which prevents me from telling him just how impossible his suit must be." She paused, then added honestly, "Though I did try once to hint to him a part of the trouble. I tried to tell him what sort of qualities I should look for in a husband. He was pleased to be amused and he told me that I should soon outgrow such nonsense."

"He told me all about that, as well," Witton said blandly.

"He told you?" Calista echoed in disbelief. Then, annoyance edging her voice, she said, "How amusing for you."

Witton shrugged and there was an edge of annoyance to his own voice as he said, "Not very. And have you outgrown such nonsense?"

Calista was looking at the road ahead of her as she replied and so she did not see the penetrating look Witton bent upon her. "Oh, I am grown far more practical these days," she said lightly. "I may read my novels as much as ever, but I am past thinking they shall one day be the stuff of my own life. And what of you? Have you never had such daydreams? Never listed to yourself the qualities you should want in a wife?"

Witton started to deny it, but then thought of Maria. With a sigh he said, "Oh, I too had my foolishness and have outgrown it. In my case I thought I had discovered such a paragon, but found, in the end, that the reality did not match the daydreams I had for her."

There was a tiny frown between her eyes as Calista said quietly, "She must have hurt you very much."

Angrily, Witton shrugged again. "It was my own fault," he said impatiently. "I should have listened to everyone who tried to tell me she was heartless and cruel and concerned only with how brilliant a match she could make. My fortune, decent as it was, made me no rival for an earl."

"Perhaps her family forced her to the match," Calista suggested with a troubled look.

Witton shook his head. "No, though they fell in, readily enough, with her scheme."

"Perhaps she really loved the earl," Calista persisted.

This time a harsh laugh greeted her reply. "Oh, no," Witton said with great assurance. "Maria left me in no doubt on that score. She was married scarcely a month before she summoned me to her side. It seemed she wished to have her cake and eat it too. I was to become her lover, the earl being some forty years older than she, you see." He paused to look at Calista, but she merely waited patiently for him to go on. Eventually he did so. "When I told her I would not, that she was married to someone else, she railed at me and told me I was cruel and did not understand the world or how it forced young women to such harsh choices. I was, I am afraid, rather blunt in expressing my disillusionment."

"The world can be cruel to young women,"

Calista said quietly. "But I cannot wonder at your anger. In fact, I begin to see why you have been so reluctant to marry since then."

She stopped and looked up at him, the frown more pronounced than ever. "John," she said, "do you really wish to marry me? Because if you don't, there is still time to cry off. There has been no notice sent to the papers and your fiancée—"

Witton cut her short by raising her free hand to his lips and kissing it. "I do want to marry you," he said firmly. "As for my fiancée, there is something I must tell you—"

Before he could tell her, however, Raynor's voice cut short their tête-à-tête. "Cal! Cal!" he called out, running toward them, "Mama wants to know if you're back yet with the ribbon she sent you for."

As he came up to them, Calista said, a trifle crossly, "Yes, of course I have the ribbon. And her silk thread. But I cannot see what is so urgent about the matter."

Raynor, who was munching on an apple, merely shrugged. Witton, holding onto his temper with an effort, said evenly, "We are headed for your house directly. But as your sister and I were discussing a matter of some importance, we wish you will go away."

"Can't," Raynor said, taking another bite of his apple.

"Don't be silly, of course you can," Calista retorted impatiently.

Raynor shook his head and grinned. "Mama saw you from an upper window and that's why she sent me out here. She said I was to stay with you, that it wouldn't look right, otherwise."

Witton muttered an oath under his breath. "Now that is the outside of enough!" he told Calista roundly. "Even your mother cannot think it improper for me to walk with you along a public road!"

"But you're not," the boy pointed out blithely. "You're on the private drive now."

"Still—" Witton began.

"I think," said Raynor wisely, as he prepared to take another bite of his apple, "that she is afraid you may take the chance to cry off."

"You may tell your mother," Witton said in measured tones, "that there is no danger of my doing so."

"You tell her," Raynor said bluntly. "She won't believe me. Besides, once I walk as far as the house with you two, I'm off to go fishing with Gil."

Witton started to issue a blistering retort to this but Calista placed a hand on his arm to forestall him. "I'll speak to mother," she said quietly. He was quick to place a reassuring hand over hers and Calista colored at his kindness. "I-I must apologize for my family," she stammered. "They are forever putting me to the blush with their frankness."

This, however, was too much for Raynor and he gave a hoot of disbelief. "We put *you* to the blush?" he demanded incredulously. "Why if that isn't a bouncer! What about all the times you've put us to the blush with your bluntness?"

"Raynor!" Witton's peremptory voice silenced the boy. Then, coolly, he went on, "However much you may bramble among yourselves, I suggest strongly, Raynor, that you and your siblings do not abuse Calista within my hearing. I warn you I shall take strong exception to your doing so."

Startled, Raynor looked at Witton with shrewd eyes and said, "So you are in love with her after all. That's all right, then. I was a bit worried, you see," he added confidingly.

"Wretch!" Calista hissed at her younger brother, mortified.

Witton merely smiled a wintery smile at the boy and observed aloud that they had reached the steps to the Standish household. "And so, my boy, you may go fishing," he said firmly.

Raynor merely grinned. "Don't get angry at me," he said frankly, "it was m'mother set me on to walk with you."

Then, before Witton could reply, he was off across the lawn toward the back buildings where he no doubt kept his fishing gear. With a chuckle, Witton took Calista's arm to mount the steps. Peeping up at him from beneath her bonnet, Calista said, a trifle uncertainly, "You—you are not angry, are you?"

Witton looked down at her anxious face and his voice softened as he said, "On the contrary, I find such honesty refreshing."

"But not such interference," Calista hazarded.

"But not such interference,"Witton agreed. He paused on the step and said earnestly, "Calista, I—"

Amabel Standish was nothing if not vigilant, however, and before he could complete the thought, she was on the top step urging them to come in. Calista could not entirely suppress a tiny gurgle of laughter at the expression on Witton's face.

He looked down at her, a twinkle in his own eyes, then. "Wretch!" he told her softly, "I shall speak with you later."

But in the hustle and bustle of the days that followed, somehow there never was a chance for Witton to have that talk with Calista. Instead, they arrived at the wedding day with perhaps too many words unspoken between them.

11

"THERE, MA'AM, I'M done," the maid said, stepping back to observe her handiwork after patting Calista's hair a final time.

Calista looked in the mirror, as her mother nodded approvingly, "Nicely done," she said. "You may go."

From a corner of the room Amethyst sniffed and said, "I daresay he won't notice the curls or her dress, anyway. Men never do."

Xanthe, who had been allowed into the room to watch only on the condition that she not cause trouble, sighed romantically and said, "I think Mr. Witton won't notice, but only because he'll be too busy looking into Calista's eyes."

At that Calista could not help but laugh. "You have been reading too many novels, I think," she said.

"Novels? Heavens, what would Papa say?" Amethyst said in mock horror.

"Oh, do give over your nonsense," Mrs. Standish said impatiently. "I haven't the time for it today. My cousin Mathilda is due to arrive at any moment, as well as the other guests, and I've got to

check with Mrs. Hastings that the tables are
already set up on the lawn, for the tenants and
villagers will be coming by later, to pay their
respects, and I will not turn them away unfed."

Mrs. Standish started toward the door of her
daughter's room, then paused and turned back.
Taking Calista's hands in her own Mrs. Standish
said, "You are a beautiful bride, Calista."

Her eyes twinkling, Calista retorted, "Hardly
beautiful, Mama. *Not* in gray. But presentable at
any rate, I daresay."

"That's what comes of getting married while
still in mourning," Amethyst said primly. "And in
haste."

Mrs. Standish hesitated a moment, then said
earnestly, "Are you altogether sure that this is
what you wish, Calista? I know it is what I have
pushed you to. Indeed, I have done everything I
could think of to make sure that Mr. Witton has
had no chance to cry off. And I wanted, still do
want, you to be married before your twenty-first
birthday, but suddenly I find myself worried, my
dear."

"Isn't that supposed to be my part?" Calista said
with a laugh.

"You may jest," Mrs. Standish said sternly, "but
I do not understand why Mr. Witton means to
marry you."

"How flattering you are, Mama!" Calista
retorted with a shaky laugh.

"That is not what I meant, and well you know

it," Amabel said severely. "We appreciate how fine a girl you are, but how can Mr. Witton? He has scarcely had time to know you."

"But Mama, he compromised her," Xanthe said wide-eyed.

Mrs. Standish rounded on her youngest daughter and said sternly, "That is enough of such nonsense from you. I will not have you saying such a thing aloud!" She turned back to Calista and said, still in a worried tone, "From what George Trumble has told me, is is no more the sort to be dictated to by any convention than you are."

Gently, Calista said to her mother, "I don't pretend to understand, Mama, why Mr. Witton has chosen to marry me, but I am very grateful that he has and it is indeed what I wish. I—I think we shall suit very well."

Impulsively, Amabel Standish hugged her daughter. "Well, my dear, all I wish is your happiness, and if you are satisfied then so am I."

Meanwhile, John Witton was answering much the same questions in his room from his friend Freddy Leverton, who had arrived late the night before.

"Now how does it come about, John," Leverton said, leaning against a dresser as he watched Witton brush his hair, "that I leave you here and within the week you are betrothed to the daughter of the house? And not content with that, set a date for the wedding that is scandalously short.

Someone might think you had compromised the poor girl or something.''

Witton set down the brush and turned to look at his friend. With a face that was expressionless he said, "I should not like to hear such a suggestion again, Freddy."

Hastily, Leverton held up his hands and said, "Come, John, I am only roasting you! The suggestion that you might have compromised a young lady's reputation is patently absurd, but you must allow me a certain curiosity. It seems so—so impetuous to me."

Witton's expression relaxed into a smile as he replied, "But why are you confused, Freddy? Didn't you have just such a notion in mind when you coaxed me to come to the Standish household and then to stay here in your place?"

"Yes, but I expected the matter to take a little longer," Leverton retorted witheringly.

Witton shrugged disarmingly as he said, "I am simply an impetuous fellow, it seems." When Leverton snorted his disbelief, Witton turned serious. "How can I explain?" he said. "I liked Miss Standish from the moment I met her and with every day I have liked her more until now I know I would not want to live the rest of my life without her."

"And Miss Standish?" Freddy asked quizzically.

"She likes me, respects me, and in time I hope will come to love me," Witton answered.

"Well, one thing is for certain," Leverton said

wryly, "her family is delighted. I wonder, however, how your mother will feel?"

Witton turned away and once more began to fuss with his already impeccably arranged neck-cloth. "My mother," he said coolly, "is forever telling me that it is my duty to wed. How can she therefore object that I have done so?"

"Your mother will," Leverton said impertinently. "Have you heard from her yet? I presume you did send her a message about the wedding?"

"Of course," Witton said, still not meeting Freddy's eyes, "but you know my mother. It will not surprise you to hear that she has chosen not to reply to my letter. And as I plan to remain here for a week or two after the wedding, it will be that long before she meets my bride and can find something to object to in Calista."

Leverton, who had strolled over to the window, now whistled and said, softly, "On the contrary, my dear fellow, I think your mother is about to find something today. It appears she's come to your wedding. With Edwin."

"The devil you say!" Witton exclaimed, pushing his friend aside to look out the window just in time to see his brother help his mother mount the front steps to the house. "But her health is not good enough to travel," he objected. "She is forever telling me so!"

"It appears," Leverton said dryly, "that your mother has made a remarkable recovery. Due, no doubt, to her overwhelming delight at the news that you were finally going to wed. You had best go down and greet her."

"Go to the devil," Witton said, but without rancor. Then, with a gleam in his eye he added, "Come along, Freddy. You are going to greet her too."

Witton seized Leverton by the arm and, before he could object, pulled him toward the doorway. With a shrug, Freddy conceded defeat and consoled himself with the thought that it would have been a pity, anyway, to miss the fireworks that were certain to ensue.

Leverton and Witton were not the only ones to be surprised. Mrs. Standish arrived at the foot of the stairs at the same moment as a servant opened the door to admit Octavia Witton and her son Edwin.

As she heard their names, Amabel hastily moved forward to greet them. "Mrs. Witton! How pleased I am that you could come to the wedding. I am Amabel Standish, Calista's mother."

Mrs. Witton greeted her hostess, then introduced her to Edwin. "Normally, of course," Mrs. Witton said faintly, "my health would not permit me to travel, but I felt this was such an extraordinary event that I must do so. Where is my other dear son, John?"

"Upstairs," Mrs. Standish replied, somewhat taken aback. "I shall send someone up to tell him you are here."

"No need, Mrs. Standish," Witton's voice came from the stairwell as he answered. "As you can see, I am here. Mama, Edwin, how are you? Does the doctor approve of your making this journey, mother?"

As Mrs. Witton greeted John with a kiss, she said aggrievedly, "As though I would miss my own son's wedding. The idea!" Then, spying Leverton still on the stairs, she added, coolly, "I see you've Leverton here with you. I shouldn't be surprised, I suppose. How are you, Frederick? And how is your wife, Eleanor? Is she here, as well?"

"My wife's doctor does not yet wish her to travel," Leverton replied easily. "Otherwise we are both perfectly well, ma'am. And yourself?"

"Well enough," she said, drawing off her gloves. "Edwin, however, is another matter. In my opinion, he ought not to have come to the wedding at all."

Not unnaturally this statement produced a certain amount of consternation, though no immediate reply. It was left to John to step into the breach and say coolly, "I collect you wished to keep Edwin from my corrupting influence?"

Someone gasped at this outrageous statement, but Mrs. Witton merely drew herself up to her full height and said coldly, "I do not particularly enjoy levity, John. You know very well that only the most extraordinary circumstances could have persuaded me to keep Edwin from attending his own brother's wedding. He fell off a horse last week, injuring his leg. It is not broken, but while neither Dr. Hedgewig nor I take a dark view of matters, we were in agreement that now was not a good time for him to undertake a journey. Edwin, however, was adamant and hence you see him here today. I trust he will not take permanent harm from doing so."

Quietly, Mrs. Standish had spoken to one of the servants and given instructions as to where Mrs. Witton and her son should be placed. Now she stepped forward to say, soothingly, "How perfectly dreadful for you, Mrs. Witton. You must have had a difficult time of it these past few days. If you would care to freshen up before the wedding, I have arranged for you to use a room on the third floor. And Edwin may share a room with my sons Gilby and Raynor. I regret I have nothing more convenient to offer you, but John did not think you would be able to come."

Mrs. Witton unbent sufficiently to say, "A room on the third floor will be perfectly adequate, I assure you. You are most kind." She paused, then added frostily, "I cannot imagine why John thought I would not come since he could not have known of Edwin's injury. But that is neither here nor there. Pray show us to the rooms, Mrs. Standish. A few moments to compose ourselves would be most welcome. Come along, Edwin."

"Oh, do let me stay and talk with John," Edwin protested.

Mrs. Witton hesitated, then said, in acid accents,

"To be sure, it is an unconscionably long time since you have seen him. Very well, John, take charge of your brother."

Witton bowed. When his mother had disappeared up the stairs, however, he turned to Edwin and smiled as he said with genuine warmth, "How are you? You look healthy, in spite of your accident."

Edwin shrugged. "Oh, that! It was nothing, really," he retorted scornfully. He paused, then said, a trifle shyly, "I hope you will be happy, John, and I look forward to meeting your bride."

John squeezed his brother's shoulder gratefully. Looking about, he realized that he, Edwin, Leverton, and an extremely interested servant were alone in the foyer. Hastily, he said, "Come, let us find Gilby and Raynor. I am persuaded you will like them."

Upstairs, Mrs. Witton pronounced herself perfectly satisfied with the small room she was to use. Then, with a slight quiver in her voice, Mrs. Witton turned to Amabel Standish and said, "Will *you* tell me what this is about?"

Mrs. Standish colored slightly as she asked cautiously, "What do you mean, Mrs. Witton?"

"This marriage," Mrs. Witton retorted impatiently. "I know something must be amiss, otherwise John would never marry in such haste or with so little notice to me."

"You will distress your son if you speak this way with him," Mrs. Standish replied gently.

"Distress him?" Mrs. Witton said indignantly. "And what do you think he has done to me? Had he any consideration for me in moving with such haste? In not troubling to come and consult with me beforehand? If nothing else, it is this appearance of something irregular I cannot like."

To Mrs. Standish's dismay, the woman then promptly burst into tears and settled onto the nearest chair to weep helplessly into her handkerchief. Her heart touched, Mrs. Standish spoke more gently as she said, "How often our children disappoint us, Mrs. Witton, and yet they still are our children, are they not? However much they may resist the notion."

Mrs. Witton dabbed her eyes. At last she said, with a sniff, "I suppose I must make my peace with John's choice. Otherwise I shall lose him completely. But I tell you frankly, Mrs. Standish, that this is not what I bargained for when I begged my son to find himself a wife."

"Nor what I bargained for," Mrs. Standish replied softly, "when *I* thought about *my* daughter's wedding day. You must excuse me, Mrs. Witton. I must go downstairs and attend to my other guests now."

And so the morning went. Xanthe, eager to convey what news she could, was the first to inform Calista that Mrs. Witton and Edwin had arrived. She was also the one to tell her mama that Cousin Mathilda was downstairs and arguing with the footman over which bedroom was to be put to her use. But it was Gilby, Raynor, and Edwin who were deputized to discover Mr. Witton's and Mr. Leverton's whereabouts when the wedding was to begin. The three boys hit it off famously. Later, neither brother could have said how it came about that Edwin was so quickly made one of the family, but he was.

Through all of it, Calista found herself calm in the face of the fears of her relatives who felt it necessary to warn her about the horrors of marriage. And Amethyst, who seemed able to express only her complaints against Mr. Trumble, was the worst of the bunch. But when they faced one another in the old family chapel, it was generally acknowledged that Calista showed an affecting assurance in wedding John Witton.

Her replies were firmly spoken and her hand scarcely trembled when he placed his ring upon her finger. If she shivered when John kissed her, no one noticed and, in any case, it was not from fear. Had Amabel Standish needed reassurance that her daughter was making the right choice, surely it was there in the warmth that filled John Witton's eyes as he gazed down at Calista and the secure way his arm guided her out of the chapel when the service was done. Not even Mr. Forster's icily disapproving stare could disquiet Calista today.

Only later, when they were alone together, did her qualms appear.

For the moment, John and Calista were to share

his bedchamber. It was not an arrangement that provided for a great deal of privacy, for the small room had been assigned to him before there had been any thought of marriage and there were a great many other bedrooms on the same floor. Still, Witton had no quarrel with the arrangement. When they removed themselves to Witton Manor there would be ample room and Calista might order the furnishings in any way she chose. At the moment he was far more concerned with the entrancing sight of his wife slowly removing the pins from her hair. She wore a shift of the finest embroidered lawn with a satin wrapper over it and Witton felt he had never seen his bride so beautiful or so vulnerable.

Seeing her husband's eyes upon her in the mirror, Calista screwed up her courage and turned to face him. Quietly she said, "What now, John?"

An amused smile upon his face, Witton moved forward and took her hand in his. "Now?" he asked with arched eyebrows. "Did your mother tell you nothing? Have your courses of learning taught you nothing?"

Calista blushed, but her voice was creditably steady as she said, "I did not mean that."

Witton continued to regard her quizzically as he said, "What, then? Where shall we live? How often do we go to London? How devoted a pair shall we be?"

"Something like that," Calista agreed with a

nod. "I know that we ought to have talked about all of this beforehand. But with Mama so vigilant there was never a chance to do so. And . . . and until this morning the notion of our marriage did not seem quite real."

"Real enough," Witton said in a husky voice as he kissed her hand and gently drew her to her feet. "Do you regret it?" he asked.

"Not I," Calista said, shaking her head.

Trembling, she did not resist as John drew her tightly into his arms and kissed her gently on the mouth. Nor did she notice when her own arms crept up about his neck and her lips parted, eager for the kisses that came hungrily as he stroked her hair. Overwhelmed by feelings she had never known before, Calista clung to John as though she felt she were drowning.

Nor did she draw away as his hands began to stroke her breasts and thighs, and she came willingly as he drew her to the bed. And then her own hands were sliding under his robe to stroke his chest in wonder. There was no haste, no fear, only John's patience and finally their mutual need.

In the end, Calista lay in his arms, the sweetest of smiles on her lips. Looking at her, John felt more happiness, more contentment than he had ever thought possible.

12

SHORTLY BEFORE NOON the next day, Mrs. Witton sought out her son John. He was walking in the garden alone, but did not seem particularly pleased at seeing his mother. "John, oh, John! There you are. I have had the most dreadful time discovering your whereabouts," she told him with a sniff.

Witton bowed politely to her and indicated a bench. "I collect you wish to speak with me?" he said expectantly.

"Wish to speak with you?" Mrs. Witton asked in shocked accents, "I should think I would! It would have been far better, far more proper, if you had come to tell me yourself of your betrothal to Miss Standish. But as you did not, I shall say nothing more on that head. You were ever a thoughtless boy and I have come to expect such Turkish treatment from you."

Witton shot his mother a cynical look before he said, mildly, "If you did not come to reproach me for the defects in my character, Mother, may I ask why you have sought me out this afternoon?"

"Why, to commiserate with you, my son, of course," Mrs. Witton replied, smoothing her skirts and carefully avoiding his eyes.

Thunderstruck, Witton asked, "What the devil are you talking about, Mother?"

"Well," Mrs. Witton said with another sniff, "I would like to believe the Standish girl feels as attached to you as you do to her, but I know about that will. And the circumstances of the fair."

With a frown John asked sharply, "How do you know about that, Mama? Edwin, I suppose. He must have had it out of Gilby or Raynor or perhaps even Xanthe."

Mrs. Witton smiled frostily at her son as she said, "On the contrary. Edwin has a regrettable tendency to view all information concerning you as something to be guarded from me. Fortunately, there are other people who understand a mother's concern, and since you did not see fit to tell me about the provisions of the will, they did. Marry by her twenty-first birthday or the girl loses ten thousand pounds. With such an inheritance at stake, one cannot blame Miss Standish for wishing to move with such haste. How convenient for her that you were at hand and willing to play the part of bridegroom. And how convenient was the accident to your curricle."

Through clenched teeth, John replied, "You very much mistake the matter, Mother. Miss Standish first refused me and even after she accepted my proposal was quite reluctant to rush into marriage. It was I who pressed for the haste."

"Clever girl," Mrs. Witton said coolly. "Perhaps I was mistaken and she is a match for you, after all. In wits, at any rate. Though she did not seem so when I spoke to her."

"You spoke to Calista?" Witton asked in a grim voice.

Mrs. Witton looked up at him, as though in surprise. "Why, of course I spoke with your bride, John, dear," she said. "It would have been most remiss of me not to speak with her and advise her."

"If you have been interfering again, Mother—" Witton began warningly.

A sob from his mother brought him up short. "Oh, John," she cried, "I cannot like the girl!" At the sight of his angry face, however, she hastened to add, "Calista is amiable enough, I grant you, but you might have looked much higher for a bride! The Wittons may not hold a title, but we rank with the best families and your fortune must make you acceptable anywhere. Why Lady Cynthia was quite willing to accept your suit, had you only pressed it, and she is the daughter of a duke!"

"I am content with my choice," he replied curtly.

"So much the gentleman, my son," Mrs. Witton said with a sigh. "But Calista! Such a lack of beauty and accomplishments. Why, she has told me herself she hasn't the slightest skill with the pianoforte! I feel for you, my son."

"As I have no interest in the instrument either, it is a matter of complete indifference to me," John said curtly.

"But John, it must be so mortifying to you to have a wife with no accomplishments," Mrs. Witton protested.

This, however, was too much for him. "No accomplishments?" he demanded incredulously. "When she reads Greek and Latin and speaks three languages? When her understanding of the Rosetta Stone rivals that of some of the best minds in England?"

Again Mrs. Witton sobbed into her handkerchief. "Oh, John, I had not meant to be so cruel as to refer to her . . . her eccentricity. And you must not," she said earnestly. "Not if you wish to bring her into society, as I am persuaded you must." He did not at once reply and Mrs. Witton smiled maliciously as she said, "You may have no notion of launching your wife's social career, but I assure you she has social ambitions. Why she has told me herself she cannot wait to be presented at court and to make the acquaintance of your friends. Her ambition is to go to London as soon as possible and begin a round of gaiety. I hope you are up to the task, John."

Irritably, Witton waved a hand. "This is absurd. It is your words you are placing in the girl's mouth. I know very well how you twist things about."

"I?" his mother asked in shocked accents. "How can you say such a thing of me? When I only have

your best interests at heart?" At his sardonic
smile, Mrs. Witton changed tactics. In soothing
tones she said, "I do hope you will be able to keep
charge of your own household, John."

"Now what the devil do you mean?" he asked
with another frown.

"Why only that Calista seems a most capable
young woman and quite accustomed to having her
own way," Mrs. Witton said innocently. "She
seems to have the habit of command."

"Excellent," Witton said shortly. "Then she will
have no trouble managing my servants."

"And you, as well?" Mrs. Witton hazarded
mildly. "There was a time when you would not
have liked to be managed. But I daresay you have
changed," she added with a sigh.

Suppressing his anger, her son managed to ask,
"When do you leave here, Mother?"

"Directly after lunch," she said. "Lady
Ponsonby is expecting me for dinner."

"Does Edwin go with you?" John asked. "I
should think he would be confoundly bored
there."

Mrs. Witton drew herself to her full height as
she replied, "Edwin has the good breeding, I
should hope, to allow himself to be amused whatever his company. However, no, he is not to
accompany me. He has asked me to leave him here
in your company and that of the Standish boys. I
do not entirely like the notion, but Mrs. Standish
has been most persuasive. You are to look after
him, mind."

"I shall," Witton agreed.

"We shall see," Mrs. Witton retorted sharply. "Now walk back to the house with me and join me for lunch, at least, before I go."

As it turned out, Cousin Mathilda meant to leave directly after lunch, also, making the exodus complete, for Leverton had left immediately after the wedding and George and Amethyst had left after breakfast the next morning. George Trumble, it seemed, had had enough of the Standish household and Amethyst finally felt up to the return trip. Everyone, of course, had had advice to impart to the newlyweds. Leverton had confined himself to advising the pair to be happy. Trumble had told John to train Calista into a proper woman.

As for Cousin Mathilda, she had eyed the pair shrewdly and said, "You won't find it easy, I'll vow, when you've both such a stubborn look about you. But I've seen worse matches succeed and succeed well. At least you've love between you, and that's more than many can say."

Mrs. Witton had been close enough to overhear and as Calista spoke with Mathilda, she said to John, for his ears alone, "Love indeed!"

"Don't you think that a useful thing?" John asked his mother mildly.

"Certainly, when a man and wife both have it," Mrs. Witton replied impatiently. "But mark my words, have a care and look sharp to your wife if you don't want to be cuckolded."

"Mother!" John said sharply, torn between

anger and disbelief that his mother would say such a thing.

But Mrs. Witton merely nodded sagely and went on, "You don't believe me, and that's natural, I suppose. What son does? But think about it, John."

With great effort John restrained himself from speaking his mind. Instead, he bowed to his mother, then said, coolly, "I had best go and see to my bride. In any event, I have no doubt you are anxious to be on your way and I shouldn't want anything to delay you."

"You aren't," his mother said brusquely. "Mind, now, I shall expect you and your wife at Witton Manor before very much time is out. If nothing else, I should think you would have the courtesy to wish to present her to your staff and they cannot be expected to come to you. In any case," she added with a distinct sniff, "you will be more comfortable in your own home. A very respectable family, the Standishes, but their house cannot be said to compare with our own!"

And upon that note Mrs. Witton turned and allowed the coachman to hand her into the carriage. John was able, however, to reply calmly, "Enjoy your visit with Lady Ponsonby, Mama, and I engage to see that Edwin keeps out of mischief."

His mother merely said disdainfully, "Since you have not been able to do so where you alone are concerned, I do not place great dependence on such a promise. However, there is no help for it.

Edwin has taken a fancy to the Standish boys and that, at any rate, is better than taking a fancy to the Standish girls. He ought, of course, to be here to say goodbye to me, but it is all of a piece that he is not. No doubt that is just the beginning of the sad influence of his being in your company and theirs."

And with that parting shot, Mrs. Witton signaled her coachman to drive on.

Witton watched for some time until the carriage was out of sight and then turned to Calista, who was waiting for him before going back inside herself.

Later that evening, as they got ready for bed, Witton paused and turned to Calista. "My dear," he said hesitantly, "do you wish to go to London?"

Immediately, Calista swung around in her chair and looked at him. "Could we?" she asked. "I have never been there, except with Papa, once, to visit Sir John Soane, and even then Papa would not take me anywhere save to museums."

Mindful of his mother's words, Witton picked at a speck of lint on his sleeve, carefully avoiding her eyes. "Are you so very eager for town parties, then?" he asked.

Calista laughed and a dimple showed in her cheek as she replied, "Indeed! What, John, did you think me a country mouse? Content to stay buried here forever? You were sadly mistaken, then. I want to go to London, to balls and routs, and be presented at court!'' she finished triumphantly.

Anyone in Calista's family would have known by the twinkle in her eyes that she was roasting John, just as she assumed he was teasing her. But Witton did not know it. Quietly, he said, "And if I told you I had a notion to retire to the country-side? I suppose you would give me no peace until you had your way?"

Jumping up from her chair to kiss his cheek, Calista laughed and said playfully, "None whatso-ever!"

Witton hesitated, his mother's words echoing more loudly than ever in his ears. But still his arms crept around Calista's waist and tightened as her lips came eagerly up to meet his. He had not looked for passion in a bride, but found it most welcome. A smile crossed his own face as he broke away long enough to look down at her and say, laughing, "Minx! I shall have to keep you close by my side or there will be a hundred fellows trying to steal you away from me."

Shyly, Calista looked up at him and said, "Oh, John, they could not!" Then, her irrepressible sense of humor took over and with a gurgle of laughter she said, "Though I don't doubt it would be very pleasant to have them try."

13

JOHN WITTON STRODE toward the dining room, humming to himself, the next morning. Calista was upstairs dressing, but Raynor and Gilby were already seated at the breakfast table. Of Mrs. Standish, Xanthe, and Edwin there was no sign.

He paused outside the door of the room to adjust his neckcloth and paused in mid-gesture as he heard Raynor say, "What do you mean to do now?"

"Ask Mr. Witton to speak to my mother about purchasing me colors," Gilby replied. "After all, now that he is our brother-in-law he cannot be said to be an outsider. Mama must listen to his opinion."

"I shouldn't bet on it," Raynor countered sardonically. "Particularly if he gets wind of how the axle on his curricle happened to give way."

Witton, who had been on the point of entering the room, having the greatest dislike of eavesdropping, did not do so. Instead, a wary frown upon his face, he listened further.

"How can he?" Gilby asked reasonably. "Not

when it's already been repaired. I own I was afraid at first that he might notice something, but as he did not . . ."

"I suppose you must be right," Raynor said doubtfully. "I still think it was a harebrained thing to do! What if he had noticed? Or someone had caught you in the act? Or if someone had been hurt?"

"No one was hurt," Gilby retorted. "And it worked."

"Yes, well, a thousand things might have gone wrong," Raynor continued. "What if they'd ridden the horses back? Or walked? Or been picked up by a neighbor? Or what if Mr. Witton simply had refused to marry Cal?"

Though he could not see it, Witton felt sure Gilby shrugged. "Then I'd have wasted my time, no worse."

"*No worse?*" Raynor exploded. "When what you've done is so—so appalling?"

"Now that is why I did not tell you beforehand what I meant to do," Gilby answered scornfully. "I knew you would be hen-hearted about the whole thing!" Then, as his brother sputtered helplessly, he went on, reminiscently, "I must say, I never thought Cal could play her part quite so well. It all hinged on that, you know."

"Do you mean Cal *knew*?" Raynor demanded incredulously. "I cannot credit that she would consent to such a scheme."

It might have been better for all concerned if

Witton could have seen Gilby's uncomfortable expression at this. But he did not. Instead, he heard what seemed to him a careless sort of laugh and the reply, "Oh, well, there was no need to spell things out for Cal. You know what a shrewd head she has, and by now I think I might know her sentiments well enough."

As he listened, stunned, Witton found his anger rising. His mother's words, though he had refused to heed them at the time, now echoed in his ears. He needed, he told himself in a sort of daze, time to think.

Instead of entering the breakfast room, he turned and left by a side door and went around to the stables. Startled by the look of rage on Witton's face, the groom hastily saddled a horse for him. When asked, hesitantly, when he might return, Witton retorted, "I don't have a devil of an idea!"

Witton rode hard and fast, jumping any hedges and fences and walls that he came to. Finally he found himself, exhausted as his horse was, by a stand of trees near a river. Slowly he dismounted and tethered the horse, patting the creature's heaving sides. Then he sat on the riverbank and threw stones into the water, cursing to himself as he did so.

Calista was in the laboratory, sorting out what would go to her new home when she left and what would stay behind for her brothers to experiment with, when John returned. His shadow fell across her and she turned to see him filling the doorway of the outbuilding. He regarded her broodingly for a long moment and she said, a troubled smile upon her own face, "John, where were you? I came down to breakfast to find you gone."

"I had some thinking to do," he said quietly. Calista hesitated and he moved forward to take her hands in his own. "Will you tell me why you married me?" he asked gravely.

Puzzled, she replied honestly, "Because you asked me to. And because I wanted to, very much."

Once more her cheek dimpled as she smiled and turned her face up as though to kiss him. Instead, Witton let go her hands and turned away. "The accident to my curricle was very convenient, wasn't it?" he asked over his shoulder.

Calista watched him fiddle with one jar and then another. "Very convenient," she agreed calmly. "Why? Are you beginning to regret that it happened?"

He turned to look at her. "Are you?" he countered.

Still confused, Calista waved a hand airily as she said, "Why, how could I be? I am married and need no longer have any fears of losing my inheritance. And to have caught *such* a matrimonial prize must be a feather in my cap!"

Something snapped in Witton's hands and the look on his face frightened her. Abruptly, Calista realized the matter was far more serious than she had guessed. At once she placed a hand on his arm and looked up into his face as she said, earnestly, "I am roasting you, John!"

"Indeed?" he said coldly. "And then what is the truth, madam?"

Bewildered, Calista looked at him, uncertain of what to say. "The truth?" she echoed. "I do not understand you."

"Very well, I shall tell you," he said curtly. "Your brother engaged himself to damage the axle of my curricle and then all of you played your parts to perfection so that I married you."

Now Calista went white with anger. "Oh, indeed?" she demanded. "I wonder that if you can credit such an outrageous notion of my family and me, you remain here!"

"I don't," he answered shortly. "I leave within the hour and I wish you to be ready to leave as well."

Calista curtsied. "I wonder, sir," she said, still white with rage, "that you ask for my company. I should have thought you would wish to be as far away from me as possible, under the circumstances."

"You mistake me, madam," Witton answered with the same white anger. "I do not desire your company. I am sending you to Witton Manor. *I* go to London."

Then, before Calista could speak further he brushed past her out of the small structure. At once Calistra gathered her skirt in one hand and ran after him. "John!" she called.

Witton halted, then slowly turned around. Impassively, he said, "Yes?"

"You cannot mean it," she said coaxingly. "Something has happened to put you out of temper, something said that you misunderstood. Tell me what it is. You cannot really wish to send me to Witton Manor while you go to London. What about Edwin?"

Evenly, Witton replied, "You are mistaken, madam. I can and I do wish to send you to Witton Manor. A carriage will be brought around for you within the hour. Edwin may go if he pleases, I suppose. But I have business in London to attend to. I leave in my own curricle as soon as I have seen you off in your carriage." He paused, then added, "As for explanations, look to your own family for those. Meanwhile, you have an hour to get ready to leave."

"But why can't I wait for you here?" Calista asked.

"Because I do not choose it," he said curtly.

By now Calista, who had meant to be calm, found her temper had been once more aroused. Holding firm her ground she said, evenly, "And suppose I do not choose to go?"

Witton bowed ironically. "I must suppose, then, that having acquired a husband, you require nothing more of me. Very well, stay here. In any event, I leave here within the hour."

He started walking again toward the house and again Calista ran after him, this time clutching his arm. "Let me go with you, John," she begged him.

Gently but firmly he detached her hand from his sleeve. Coldly he said, "Thank you, no. I will not have you in London cutting up my peace."

"But I am your wife!" Calista protested.

"Then behave as my wife," he told her coldly. "Go to Witton Manor and wait for me to return."

"I will not," she said, in a voice as cold as his own. "Not so long as you cannot or will not give me good and sufficient reason to do so."

Once more he bowed ironically to her and then walked away. This time Calista did not try to stop him, but instead headed for the outbuildings in search of her mother. She found her in the laundry room with the new girl. Acutely aware of the interested stares of the laundry staff she said, "Mama, John finds he must leave at once. A family emergency, I collect."

Startled, Mrs. Standish said, "The laundry can wait. I shall go back to the house with you and see that the essentials, at least, are packed. What will you need to take?"

Calista waited until they were out of earshot before she replied. "I shan't need anything, Mama, I am staying here."

Mrs. Standish came to an abrupt halt. "Staying here?" she repeated. "Whatever can you mean? Of course you are going with your husband."

Resolutely, Calista shook her head. "John is leaving within the hour and I am staying here."

"But why?" her mother all but cried. Then,

sharply, Mrs. Standish added, "You've quarreled, the pair of you, haven't you?" Numbly, Calista nodded and her mother went on, in the same sharp voice, "Well, you've got to patch it up then." As Calista tilted her chin obstinately up into the air, Mrs. Standish said sternly, "Now, Calista, every young couple quarrels. Why your father and I did so on our wedding night. But it means nothing! Come, patch up your quarrel with John and have done with it. Your place is at your husband's side."

"Tell John that," Calista said with a derisive laugh.

With a sigh Mrs. Standish said, "I suppose that means I shall have to coax the story out of you."

Miserably, Calista shrugged her shoulder. "Oh, by all means I am willing to be frank with you. Why not? We quarreled because John came and told me to be packed and ready to leave within the hour."

"Vexing, to be sure," Mrs. Standish put in at once. "Men simply don't understand how long it takes to pack. But he will. Just tell him you need more time."

It was Calista's turn to sigh. "Mama," she said gently, "John wanted me to pack to be ready to go to Witton Manor while he goes directly to London."

"Nonsense! You must have misunderstood him," her mother said stoutly.

"I wish I had," Calista said evenly, "but John

left me in no doubt that that is exactly what he meant."

"I shall speak to him," Mrs. Standish said determinedly. "A wife's place is at her husband's side. You must have offended him, somehow. I shall do my best to smooth things over, but in the future you must be more careful."

Incensed, Calista replied, "And if I had offended John? Is that a reason for him to behave in such a manner? Shouldn't he have told me why he was angry? Perhaps he is the one who should be more careful in the future."

"Calista!" her mother remonstrated. "You must not talk that way. However hard it may seem to you, nevertheless, you know very well that it is your responsibility to see that there is no rift between you and John. Where would we have been if I had caviled at all your father's eccentricities? Now come along and let me find John."

At the house Witton condescended to speak with Mrs. Standish, but not in the slightest would he be swayed either to alter his decision or to explain the reasons for it. At the end of the stipulated hour he was ready to leave. Calista stood with her mother on the steps to bid him goodbye.

Pulling his gloves between his hand, Witton addressed her one more time. "Well, Calista?" he asked sternly. "Will you go to Witton Manor? There is still time to order the carriage brought around."

"I will not," she answered in a clear voice.

"Oh, but dear, perhaps you ought to," her mother began.

"No," Calista said implacably.

Witton bowed. Then he turned to Mrs. Standish and said, "I pray you will say goodbye to your sons for me. And to Edwin. The scamp is nowhere to be found. Oh, and Mrs. Standish, I suggest that you waste no time in purchasing a commission for your eldest son. Otherwise, I very much fear he is going to land himself in serious trouble with pranks of one sort or another before he is very much older!"

Before she could reply he had climbed into his curricle, where his valet was waiting for him. Not by the slightest twitch of his eyes or mouth did that fellow betray how astonishing it was to him to be ordered to leave at such short notice or to ride in his master's curricle rather than a chaise, as was more usual. Nor did Witton explain. Instead, as they pulled away from the house and turned down the drive, Witton merely said, in the same curt voice he had used with everyone else, "I don't wish to talk about it. In fact, I don't wish to talk at all."

"Very good, sir," the valet said, taking great care to stare straight ahead.

Meanwhile, as the carriage pulled away from the house and down the drive, Calista stared bleakly after it. In vain, she tried to recall the events of the day and night before in an attempt to puzzle out how her husband could have come to believe what he did. In the end she could not, and Gilby and Raynor were not around to enlighten her.

14

It WAS AN extraordinarily sober group who gathered in the drawing room that evening. Mrs. Standish was not there. Xanthe had caught some childhood complaint and while not gravely ill, was crotchety enough to have called for the presence of her mother. That left Gilby, Raynor, and Edwin to sit with Calista after dinner.

"Have you no notion why he went haring off to London without you?" Edwin asked with a frown. "It seems extraordinarily unlike John."

Calista sadly shook her head. Too restless to sit still, she paced about the room before she spoke. "None," Calista replied at last. "At least, none beyond some strange thing he said. Something to the effect that now that I had the husband I craved I no longer needed him. And that the accident to his curricle was no accident. But what could have given him such a notion as that? He was not in such a mood when I sent him down to breakfast this morning."

There was a stunned silence in the room before

Raynor carefully said, "Breakfast? About what time, Cal?"

She shrugged impatiently, "Nine, nine-thirty, ten, what can it signify?"

"A great deal," Gilby said significantly. "As we told you when you came down this morning, we never saw him but—"

"But what?" Calista demanded.

Raynor cleared his throat. "You aren't going to like this," he warned her.

"Not like it?" Calista demanded in exasperation. "What has that to say to the matter? I want to know what caused such a change in my husband!"

"We did," Gilby said in a small, miserable voice.

"You did?" Calista said incredulously. "How?"

There was another long, uncomfortable silence. At last Raynor said quietly, "Gilby and I were talking about something. Perhaps John overheard. I don't think he would have liked it. And I don't think Edwin will if he hears it either."

"Overheard what?" Calista asked. When they still hesitated she added ominously, "You'd best tell me now. Sooner or later I am bound to find out, you know. As for Edwin, if John knows he may as well."

Raynor looked at Gilby, who appeared to find his neckcloth suddenly too tight for he strained his chin against it before he said, "I, that is, it's my fault, Cal. I knew you and Mr. Witton were suited, but the pair of you didn't. So I tried to help things along a bit."

"Help things along?" Calista prompted grimly when he faltered and stopped speaking.

"At the fair. You remember, the axle of his curricle broke," Gilby said at last.

"I am scarcely likely to forget it," Calista replied, "considering the consequences."

"Well, but that's it," Gilby said eagerly. "I knew that if I found a way to throw the pair of you together, it would answer. Particularly since I could tell Mr. Witton was a gentleman and would do the right thing."

"And it did answer," Raynor pointed out helpfully. "You two are married."

"Yes, with my husband on his way to London and myself here!" Calista all but shouted at him. Then, recollecting herself, she said grimly, but more quietly, "Do you mean, Gilby, that you tampered with his carriage? And that you, Raynor, approved? Were involved as well? That John overheard the pair of you boasting about the whole thing? No wonder he was furious! And I denied it, not believing the pair of you—or anyone —were capable of such infamy," she concluded bitterly.

"Acquit me," Raynor said hastily, "I'd not the full knowledge of what Gil had done either until this morning. But yes, that is what we're afraid he may have overheard."

Feeling a trifle overwhelmed, Calista sank into the nearest chair. She looked at Edwin, who had gone quite pale, and said in a voice that was full of constraint, "I cannot blame you if you would choose to leave as well."

Edwin did not at once answer. After a long moment he said, "It is appalling and I can well imagine what John felt when he discovered he'd been served such a turn. But I shan't leave. Not just yet, at any rate." He paused, then added, "Were it anyone but you that John had been forced into marrying, I should be as furious as he is. But as it is, I can understand the impulse that prompted Gilby to act as he did."

"Well, that is certainly more than I can say," Calista retorted. Then, her face still pale with shock, she said to him, "What do I do now? Like you, I cannot blame John for being furious. Yet how can I hope to convince him that I had no part in this?"

"Are you sure that he thinks you did?" Edwin asked.

"Probably," Gilby said miserably. "If he heard the rest, he may have also heard me say that Cal played her part well."

"You claimed I knew?" Calista demanded incredulously.

"That's what I asked," Raynor said, "and Gil replied there had been no need to spell it out for you."

Numbly Calista turned to Edwin. "Ought I to write and tell John I am coming to London anyway? Ought I to just go? Perhaps if I did, he would listen to me there," she said.

"I shouldn't think so," Edwin said gloomily. "Ten to one he'd only think you're behaving like my mother: trying to bully him into doing what you want him to do."

"What am I to do, then?" Calista cried, rising to her feet and beginning to pace about the room again, twisting her lace handkerchief in her hands. "I cannot simply sit here waiting for John to come back to me. He may never do so."

After a moment Edwin said, uncertainly, "John's my older brother and perhaps I'm wrong to try to advise you. After all, I don't see him all that often these days since my mother won't let me go to London and John doesn't visit Witton Manor above once a year. But I do know my mother and what she's been about all these years.

"In your shoes I should write and tell John you understand his position and don't mean to push or pry, that he may do as he wishes. If you try to push or pull at John or convince him of anything by rational means, it won't serve. He's had a lifetime of that sort of pinching and nagging from our mother and nothing is more certain to turn him up sharp," Edwin continued.

"Let John see that you are not pining for him, for if there is one thing he cannot abide it is to have someone forever clinging to his arm. I swear it is the reason he does not visit Witton Manor more. My mother is an expert at strangling one with her affections," Edwin concluded.

"Yes, but won't that just convince him he was

right?" Calista demanded impatiently. "Perhaps if I went to him and told him the true story he might listen."

Edwin nodded. "He might think it confirmed his opinion. At first. But he'd come about. Faster than if you went to London. John needs time to cool down and to discover how much he misses you. John doesn't anger easily, but when his temper's aroused it's hard for him to forgive. But if he thinks he might be losing you, he's much more likely to listen to what you have to say." Edwin paused, then added thoughtfully, "Why don't we all go to Bath in the meantime?"

Calista stared at John's younger brother and even Gilby and Raynor gaped in disbelief. "Are you roasting Cal?" Gilby asked suspiciously.

"You've got even more windmills in your head than Gil does!" Raynor said angrily.

"Not a bit of it," Edwin said indignantly. "Why not go? It will certainly show John she doesn't mean to hang about moping over him, and believe me, nothing could be more fatal than for him to think that. And besides, I've never been much of anywhere. Mama has kept me shut up at home all these years. Surely you can understand how that might chafe a fellow," he said, appealing to Gilby.

Grudgingly, Gil nodded and even Raynor reluctantly allowed that, "I'd just as soon Witton not think my sister's pining over him. Serve him right if he gets upset or if she meets someone better in Bath. He oughtn't to have been such a

gudgeon as to stomp out of here without finding
out the whole story from all of us."

Still Calista hesitated. "C'mon, Cal," Gilby
coaxed. "You know the only time we've been to
Bath has been with Papa to study the history.
We'd have a far more amusing time with you than
that. And with Xanthe sick, it is our best chance to
go without Mama."

"And it cannot be thought improper," Edwin
said coolly, "for you're almost one and twenty and
are a married woman now and Gil and Ray are
your brothers and even I'm related since your
marriage to John."

Calista turned her back on all of them to stare at
the drafty fireplace that now stood empty of com-
forting flames. At last she said, "I cannot.
However hurt I may be by John, I cannot serve
him such a turn. There would be bound to be
gossip, you know there would. I have already
served him an evil turn through what you did."
Sharply she rounded on Gilby. "If only you had
thought to come and ask me what I wanted! Or
what I knew. Don't you understand? John had a
lady he was all but formally pledged to. How do
you think she feels now?"

Gilby had the grace to look more abashed than
ever, as did Raynor. Edwin, however, startled
them all by saying, in a puzzled voice, "What are
you talking about, Calista?"

"The—the woman John was all but engaged to,"
Calista repeated. "John told me about her
himself."

Edwin leaned back in his chair and said, "Sounds like a hum to me. Aside from someone years ago, who is married, I've heard of no one catching John's eye until now. My mother had begun to give up hope he'd ever marry. Not that he didn't have his bits of muslin, of course, but that's another thing entirely. Ten to one he just said that so none of you would try to matchmake. John doesn't like matchmaking, you see," he concluded ingenuously.

"Yes, well, he said it to the wrong person, then, didn't he," Gilby said dryly.

Calista, who had been standing quite still, now let out a deep breath before she said, grimly, "So it was all a hum? So I did not then take him away from another woman? He made no such sacrifice for me after all?"

"Well, I could be wrong, of course," Edwin said cautiously, "but I don't think so. Even if John hadn't told me what was afoot himself, one of his servants would have had wind of such a female and my mother has had them all in her pay these past five years and more. And she would have told everyone about it, you may be sure."

Slowly, Calista sat down. Edwin watched her silent ruminations with interest and Gilby and Raynor with foreboding, for they knew their sister only too well. At last Calista looked up and addressed the three young men in a calm, agreeable voice. "I think, Gil, Ray, that it is time your education was extended to include a social visit to Bath. And you, Edwin, may certainly come along as well."

"What do you mean to do, Cal?" Raynor asked warily.

"Do?" Calista repeated grimly. "Why I mean to do just as Edwin suggests. I shall show my husband that I do not mean to sit at home and pine over his absence. I shall go to Bath and enjoy myself. If Mama allows it."

"And the gossip?" Raynor persisted quietly.

Calista regarded her brother bleakly as she replied, "If there is gossip, let my husband wonder how to handle it. It is, after all, his choice that we are separated so soon after our marriage."

Fortunately, Mrs. Standish did not walk in at that moment, but some ten minutes later when the conversation was unexceptionable. While she did not altogether like the scheme proposed, she did give her consent.

"I can understand your wish to visit Bath and have some fun," she told the four. "I wish I could take you myself. But Xanthe has just begun to throw out spots and I am convinced it is the measles. I cannot think where she could have contracted them, but it is all of a piece that she has done so now. And I cannot leave her to go to Bath with you."

"Surely you do not forbid us to go there with Cal," Raynor said coaxingly.

Mrs. Standish hesitated and Gilby added, "She *is* almost twenty-one, Mama. And a married woman."

"I know it," Mrs. Standish agreed reluctantly.

"And your Papa did feel strongly that one ought to allow children as much freedom as possible. Very well, I suppose it can do no harm. Particularly if Mr. Forster advises you on where to put up and such."

At this Gilby and Raynor groaned but Edwin immediately said, gravely, "Certainly he shall do so, if you wish, Mrs. Standish."

"But mind, you are to listen to your sister," Mrs. Standish warned her sons.

"We may go, then?" Calista asked anxiously.

"Yes, you may go," Mrs. Standish said with a sigh.

15

A WEEK LATER, in London, John Witton found himself still angry. He had received, that morning, a letter in the post from Calista. It had not improved his temper in the least and so, by mid-afternoon, he found himself calling upon the Levertons at their townhouse. He was, Eleanor informed him cheerfully, just in time to see her young son being sent off to the nursery for a much-needed nap. Unfortunately, the sight of the gurgling infant only lowered his spirits further. With a perceptive look at his friend's face, Freddy Leverton took Witton's arm and led him into the library, with Eleanor promising to follow as soon as she had seen the baby tucked in upstairs.

For several minutes the two men talked of trivialities. Then, when Eleanor entered the room, she altered matters by asking bluntly, "Have you heard from Calista, John?"

"Probably," Leverton told his wife with a teasing smile. "John seems remarkably restless today."

"I don't like that smile of yours, Freddy,"

Witton retorted frankly. "It reminds me too much of Lord Alvanley asking when he may look to meet my bride."

"Surely you cannot be surprised at that," Eleanor said gently. "Everyone has been so long accustomed to thinking of you as forever single that they can scarcely imagine you so bowled over by a girl that you would marry her out of hand. And while she was still in mourning. Then, as though that were not astonishing enough, you reappear in London without your bride. Romance would be one thing, but now they have scented a mystery as well. Of course they are curious to meet Calista!" She paused, then added mildly, "When, by the by, *do* you mean to bring her to town? I warn you, the doctor may give me leave to travel any day now, and if you do not bring her to meet me, I may go to see her."

"I cannot," Witton replied shortly, "since I do not, at the moment, know where Calista is!"

"What?" the pair exclaimed.

"Well, not precisely, at any rate," Witton amended. He paused, then said, his voice devoid of emotion, "I had a letter from Calista today. She writes to tell me that she will put no pressure upon me to return to her side. She will, she says, instead take herself off to Bath and send me her direction there when she knows it."

"What the devil does she mean by that?" Leverton asked with a frown.

"I think it tolerably clear," Witton said coldly.

"It is just such a letter as Maria might have written, after all."

Startled, Leverton protested. "I know you are angry at Calista," he said, "though why, you will not tell us. But still, surely you are too harsh on the girl! Recollect that I have met her and I saw nothing of Maria in Calista then."

"That is because you do not know the whole of it!" Witton retorted sharply.

"Why not tell us then?" Eleanor asked gently. "You are more like family than friend to us, you know."

"Because, madam, I do not like to advertise my folly," he said frostily.

Eleanor only laughed. "Now don't try coming it top-lofty with me," she warned him severely, "I know you far too well." She paused, then added coaxingly, "Please tell us, John. You know that Freddy and I cannot like to see you in such distress."

For a very long time Witton was silent. At last, reluctantly, he nodded. "Very well. I do not deny that I liked Calista very much, from the first day I met her," he said quietly. "Even had nothing occurred I might, in time, have decided to make her my wife. But fate, or so I thought it at the time, intervened. On the way back from some country fair my curricle broke down, the horses bolted, and it was pouring rain. Calista and I were forced to take shelter overnight, alone, in a deserted barn somewhere."

Eleanor hissed as she said, "I see, so you married her out of duty."

"Yes. No. I scarcely know now," Witton said, running a hand through his already somewhat disheveled hair. "To be sure, it would have been the act of a cruel man to have refused to marry Miss Standish after that. And yet I might have done so had I held her in dislike. But I did not. Fool that I was, I thought I was in love with Calista."

"You certainly seemed to be, the day of the wedding," Freddy said quietly. "And you do not seem free of her yet."

"I am not," John replied shortly. "A hundred times a day, it seems, I find myself turning to share something with Calista only she is not there."

"But why not?" Eleanor demanded impatiently. "It is not, after all, her fault that your curricle broke down. And you say yourself you wanted to marry her."

"Ah, but it is her fault," John retorted, looking his hostess steadily in the eye. "Or her brother's, at any rate," he amended, after a moment. "I heard both her brothers boasting a few days after the wedding. They were talking about how the elder one had arranged the accident. And of how well Calista played her part as the reluctant bride-to-be."

An appalled silence fell upon the room and it was some time before anyone ventured to break it.

At last John said quietly, "Perhaps it is a blessing that Calista has chosen to go to Bath. There are any number of tattleboxes who will delight in informing me of her behavior. And if I find that she is like Maria, that she does surround herself with flirts, why then perhaps I will find it easier to take the steps to dissolve our marriage."

"Did—did she admit to you what had happened?" Eleanor asked in a small voice. "Is it possible that she did not know what her family had done?"

Witton shrugged. "Perhaps," he admitted reluctantly. "That is one of the fears that has haunted my days. That I have misjudged her. But then there is her letter. It does not sound, I think, as though she pines for my company."

He paused and looked at Eleanor, who said in a troubled voice, "It is a cold-sounding letter, I own. And yet I cannot help but wonder if it is her hurt pride that made your wife write as she did. You do not know how much it may have cost her to write those words that give you such distress. It is so easy to write words one does not mean."

"Perhaps," Witton repeated quietly.

"What do you mean to do?" Eleanor asked, in the same troubled voice as before.

He looked at her and said, coolly, "I think I shall go for a ride in the park. Care to come, Freddy?"

Witton rose, and the others did so as well. Eleanor placed a hand on his sleeve and John covered it with his own. In answer to the unspoken protest in her eyes he said with a sigh, "I don't know. Wait and hope that some solution offers itself to me. God knows I still love Calista!"

"Good lord!" Calista said expressively as she looked around the small private parlor at the inn the Standish party had arranged to put up at during their stay in Bath.

"Just so,"Raynor agreed grimly.

"I knew you oughtn't to have trusted it to the vicar," Gilby said hotly. "I knew we should do better to put up at the White Hound."

"Oh, do give over," Calista said repressively. "You know Mama would never have allowed us to come if we had not allowed Mr. Forster to choose an inn for us. However little she may like him or respect his intelligence, though even so I must say I think she overestimated him, Mama felt it would not do for us to hare off on our own or hire a house without a chaperone or put up at a sporting place, which I collect the White Hound to be. Look at Edwin, you do not see him complaining."

"That is because I am far too polite," the boy said impishly.

"There, you see!" Gilby crowed triumphantly.

Calista sighed and walked over to the window. "To be sure," she said in a small voice, "it is not quite what I had hoped for. The rooms are small, the furnishings entirely undistinguished, and the location shabby genteel."

"Yes, just what a vicar might be expected to

choose for himself," Gilby could not resist adding. "Why don't we leave here?" he pleaded. "It's not as though we've signed a lease or anything."

"Oh, Gil, it would look like such a rudeness to Mr. Forster," Calista said doubtfully. She paused, then added, "And yet, I own I cannot like this place."

It was left to Edwin to clinch the matter. "John will never believe you are amusing yourself to any purpose here if you puff off to him so unfashionable an address as this."

"Oh, and just where do you suggest we stay?" Calista demanded.

Edwin shrugged. "I don't know, but I can tell you who does. My Aunt Grace lives here in Bath and while she must be almost sixty, she's bang up to the mark on fashion. Puts even my mother into a fever when she comes to call because she knows what's proper and what ain't and what's all the crack."

"You have an Aunt Grace here and you didn't think to tell us before now?" Calista asked in an awful voice.

Edwin shrugged again and grinned engagingly. "Tell the truth, I was rather hoping we could avoid Lady Carsby—that's my aunt—for as long as possible. She does have the knack of making one feel as if one were still in short pants. But ten to one she could tell us what to do."

Calista thought a moment, then nodded decisively. "Very well, we shall consult your Aunt

Grace. And I hope we may be in a new place before tomorrow."

This pronouncement was greeted with cheers and statements to the effect that Calista was a "right'un" and a "great gun." As she well knew these pronouncements would not last past their next falling out with her, Calista gave these shouts of approval no more weight than they deserved.

Calista was by no means persuaded that they ought to all drive around and descend upon Edwin's Aunt Grace unannounced, even though that was what he advised. Instead, borrowing stationery from the inn where they were putting up, Calista sent a civil note indicating that Edwin was in Bath in her care and begging the favor of a visit in order to ask advice. The reply was brought back by hand within half an hour that Calista was to present herself, without delay, in Great Pulteney Street, with Edwin in tow.

Neither Gilby nor Raynor expressed disappointment upon being informed that they would not take part in the visit to Lady Carsby. "It is bad enough to have me suddenly appear," Calista said severely. "I will not inflict the pair of you upon her as well."

"Excellent notion," Gilby agreed. "Ten to one she would look at us and decide she didn't like us and then where would we be. But mind, now, don't let her fob off some fancy but dull address upon us. We want to be in the midst of things."

With a tiny sigh Calista said, "I shall do my best.

I only hope that I can contrive not to offend the woman. You know how dreadfully my tongue can run way with me at times."

Calista's first view of the house in Great Pulteney Street did nothing to reassure her. It was furnished in the first stare of elegance, an elegance matched by its owner. Lady Carsby wore a dress of orange crape that would have been becoming on a woman of five and twenty and yet she somehow contrived not to look ridiculous. And the cap she wore on her head was far more dashing than any other woman her age would have thought proper. By comparison, Calista felt distinctly dowdy in her carriage dress of gray bombazine trimmed with black crape and matching bonnet.

The only circumstance that was in the least reassuring was that Edwin and Cal found her waiting for them alone, having dismissed her usual afternoon callers.

Still, it was daunting to have Lady Carsby begin by demanding, "What the devil are you doing with my great-nephew Edwin here in Bath, young woman? Aren't you a mite old for him?"

Smoothly, Calista dropped a curtsy before taking the chair her hostess pointed her to. Then, with a calm she did not entirely feel, she replied, "As I am Edwin's sister-in-law, I cannot think it too unreasonable for me to have his company in traveling to Bath."

"Sister-in-law!" Lady Carsby repeated, startled. "Never say you've married John Witton?"

Amused in spite of herself, Calista asked, "Is there any reason why I should not have?"

"No, no, none," Lady Carsby replied with a frown. "On his side, at any rate. I like and respect John. It's you I know nothing about. Why didn't your mother write and tell me about it, young man?" Lady Carsby demanded, pointing at Edwin.

He shrugged. "I must suppose she did but that the letter hasn't yet arrived."

"Hasn't yet arrived?" Lady Carsby repeated. "When did this wedding take place?"

"Last week," Calista said meekly.

"Last week!" Lady Carsby exploded, reaching for her hartshorn. "And you are here in Bath with Edwin? Coming it much too strong, my dear, much too smoky by half. Where's John, and why isn't he here with you?"

This was the question Calista had dreaded having to answer and she did not do so now. Instead, Edwin leapt into the fray. "You know what John is," he said, cheerfully sacrificing his brother's character. "He took a pet over some small thing and hared off to London. Rather than rusticate I suggested to m'sister-in-law that she come to Bath and take her mind off her troubles."

Lady Carsby snorted in disbelief. She then proceeded to tick off the points on her fingers as she replied, "Number one, no, I don't know what John is like if he'd take a pet over something unimportant. What's more, I don't believe it.

Number two, why shouldn't his wife rusticate until he came to his senses? Number three, even if she did think the quickest way to bring him to heel was to show him she could have a good time without him, why bring you along to Bath?"

"To keep my own brothers company," Calista offered meekly.

Lady Carsby stared at Calista for a long moment before she said, "Your brothers?"

"Gilby and Raynor," Edwin explained helpfully.

"Why bring them?" Lady Carsby persisted, continuing to stare at Calista.

"For company. Because they've not been here before, except on scholarly tours with my father. Because . . . because they begged me to and I could not say no," Calista answered honestly.

For a long moment there was silence. Then, at last, Lady Carsby said slowly, "Very well, what do you want of me?"

"Advice. My mother asked our vicar to suggest an inn for us to stay at, a place that he has used when visiting Bath with his mother. But—"

"But the place wouldn't suit," Lady Carsby cut Calista short, ruthlessly. "It wouldn't. You needn't tell me about vicars, I know," she said sourly. "So you want advice on where to seek lodgings?"

Again Edwin answered for Calista. "We want John to think Cal's settled in here and enjoying herself. That she isn't pining for his company even though she is. And I knew you could tell us what would be both a fashionable and a lively place to stay."

Lady Carsby laughed, but not kindly. "I won't say I think your scheme will work, but it ought to be amusing to watch," she said. "Very well, I'll help you. Go around to number twenty-five Gay Street. A lady named Mrs. Haverton takes in lodgers and I happen to know that she is in need of some now. She will engage to provide you with clean, well-furnished rooms including a private parlor, and tidy meals, and she'll stay out of your way otherwise entirely."

"You're very kind," Calista began doubtfully.

"Very kind, but you want to know more about the place first?" Lady Carsby suggested with another laugh. "Don't worry. Mrs. Haverton is an old acquaintance of mine and had her husband not been so improvident she would never have been reduced to such shifts. But she is as I have described her. You will find that she has her own friends and will not try to insert herself into your affairs. Moreover, she has excellent taste, if a limited budget, and you will find the furnishings pleasing if not in the latest mode. And the address is close in to the center of the city. You and your brothers won't want to be depending on chairmen or walking forever when you spend an evening at the assembly rooms or the other, less respectable haunts I've no doubt your brothers will seek out. Never fear, I know what I'm about."

She paused, then added shrewdly, "And even if I

didn't, you'd only need to take a look at the place
and say you don't like it. You needn't fear I'll take
a pet. Now go and get settled in, assuming you like
the place, and meanwhile I'll pass the word to my
younger acquaintances and their parents that my
great-nephew's wife is in town."

Alarmed, Calista started to rise as she said,
"That's another thing, Lady Carsby, that I hadn't
quite settled. Should I use John's name? Or my
unmarried name? So few people know we were
married. If John should decide he—he wants to be
rid of me, won't it make matters harder if I use his
name now?"

"I don't doubt it," Lady Carsby said curtly. "Is
that what you want? My great-nephew to set aside
the marriage?"

Calista was very pale and her voice faint as she
shook her head and said, "No. But—"

"But nothing!" Lady Carsby said sternly. "I like
you, my girl, and that's more than I can say about
most of my own family. I'll help you. And not just
with advice. Let there be talk about Mrs. John
Witton. It's bound to reach John in London and if
nothing else he'll post down here to stop you from
stirring up a scandal. And once we have him at
your side, why I'll trust to your common sense and
my experience to bring him around. Though mind,
if I find there is some reason for him to be better
off without the match, I won't hesitate to help him
end it," Lady Carsby warned.

With a wry smile Calista replied, "I think I'll
take that chance, Lady Carsby."

"Good for you. Now go and try to keep this scapegrace great-nephew Edwin of mine out of too much trouble."

"I shall try," Calista answered with a curtsy.

16

By THE END of their first day in Bath, Gilby, Raynor, Edwin and Calista were settled into a set of rooms with a private parlor at number 25 Gay Street. As Lady Carsby had said, it was in the heart of Bath and comfortable to boot. Mrs. Haverton, moreover, was all that Lady Carsby had said she would be. She had expressed herself delighted to be able to accommodate relations of her ladyship and, after showing them the tidy set of rooms she had set aside for lodgers and arranged for their meals, she had whisked herself out of sight. Even the boys' newly acquired valet and Calista's maid pronounced themselves better pleased with the lodgings than they had been with the inn.

After seeing that all their baggage was suitably stashed away in their rooms, the four gathered in the private parlor for tea.

Edwin watched the passersby from the window, then turned and crowed with delight. "We are here, actually here! It will be beyond anything famous, Calista. You will not regret coming to Bath, I promise you."

Calista was amused. "I suppose so," she said. "Though I had not thought Bath such a famous place for sport. I have rather heard it described as a place for quizzes to come and take the waters."

Edwin turned away quickly, but it seemed to Calista that he colored a trifle as he said, off-handedly, "Oh, there is more to the place than that. Not all of which would be appropriate for you, of course. But don't worry, we shan't shab off, your brothers and I, from escorting you to the assemblies. Or to the pump room."

"Here, now," Gilby said in alarm, "that's not all we mean to do."

"Not by any means," Raynor seconded with a vigorous nod of his head.

"Nor do we mean to let you drag us off to see the historical sights," Gilby warned ominously.

Calista could not help but laugh. "Peace," she said. "I've no more desire to see those than you do. I should think Papa did as thorough a job as can be imagined educating us as to Bath's historical points of interest when he brought us five years ago." She paused, then added, "But I should like to go to the assembly tomorrow night."

Gilby and Raynor groaned, but Edwin immediately said, "We shall be glad to go with you. Tonight, though, your brothers and I may take a walk about the town. You'll be too tired from the journey to want to do anything anyway, I daresay," he concluded with an innocent air.

Calista was not deceived. "By that I collect you

mean to kick up a lark or do something that your mother and mine would not approve of. Still, I am not your guardian."

Edwin was amused. "You scarcely could be," he said, "when you and I are all but the same age." At her sharp look he added, a trifle sheepishly, "Well, you've not above two years on me, at any rate. Or on Gilby. As for Raynor, you may be sure we shall not let him fall into any scrape. Come, we are more likely to fall into a scrape if you try to hem us in too close playing nursemaid."

With a tiny sigh Calista replied, "I cannot help but think you may be right. Gil and Ray are never in so much trouble as when Mama has tried to keep them away from it. Very well, go out and enjoy yourselves."

That pronouncement brought a rousing cheer down upon Calista's head. When it was over, she smiled and merely said quietly, "You are quite right, Edwin, in thinking I shall want to seek my own bed early tonight. The jolting of the traveling coach has taken a greater toll on me than I would have thought possible."

"That's what comes of hiring a carriage cheaply," Gilby said with a snort of disgust.

"Yes, but you could not expect Mama to send us in hers, with the coachman," Calista replied reasonably. "How would she have gotten about? And there was no better establishment to hire a chaise from anyway."

"I know," Gilby muttered, "but I still wish we

hadn't cut such comical figures arriving in such a shabby way."

"Oh, no one will have taken notice of us," Raynor told his brother carelessly. "And when we leave we may hire as neat a setup as we please."

The next morning, after a leisurely breakfast, Gilby and Raynor reluctantly agreed to accompany Calista to the pump room, at Edwin's urging. If she suspected that her brothers might have enjoyed themselves a trifle too well the night before she did not say so. Instead, she donned a dark blue pelisse over a similarly colored dress and a dark bonnet and pronounced herself ready to depart the inn. Her brothers, of course, tried to tell her she looked too dowdy, but Calista was firm in her resolve.

"You know we must still be considered to be in mourning, Gil, Ray, whatever Papa may have thought of the custom. And I will not set up people's backs by flouting that custom. Certainly not at the start of our stay here."

"Oh, very well," Gilby grumbled. "Though if you meant to be such a stick in the mud we might just as well have stayed at home."

Fortunately, Edwin stepped into the breach and demanded to know if they intended to spend every moment of their stay in Bath brangling.

It was only a short walk to the assembly rooms, where Calista inscribed their names in the subscription books. "For depend upon it, this is where everyone will be of an evening," she told her brothers.

"It looks deucedly flat to me," Gilby protested.

Edwin, however, was of a different opinion and said, "I disagree. And in any event, if Cal wishes to have any success in convincing my brother she has forgotten him, she must be seen to be cutting a dash, and in Bath that means attending all the assemblies. Even if she don't mean to dance."

Afterward they walked to the pump room just off the Abbey Courtyard. There the four drank the waters and uniformly pronounced them ghastly, though not so loudly that anyone else could hear. And finally capped the morning with a visit to the Parade Gardens where even Gilby was moved to comment that Bath was a splendid place after he noticed a number of small boats on the river and learned where he could rent one.

"You must come with us, Cal," Raynor said exuberantly. "It will be beyond anything great!"

"Particularly since you have never been in a boat before in your life," Calista agreed cordially.

"But that will simply make it more of an adventure," Gilby said eagerly.

"Won't we be a trifle crowded?" Edwin asked doubtfully, watching a boat go by.

"To be sure, you would be crowded with me along," Calista said quickly. "I assure you I would be content to return to Gay Street. I must write John a letter giving him our direction, anyway. Mrs. Haverton has engaged to see that it is posted as soon as I have done so."

It took little more to persuade the boys although they did insist on escorting her back to their lodgings before setting out for the river. "For it won't do to have you wandering about these streets all alone," Gilby said frankly. "And I don't trust these chairmen not to take you out of the way and charge you extra for doing so."

Back in Gay Street, Calista sat at the little writing desk near the window and tried to compose a letter to Witton. It was not in her nature to easily take the advice of others and she could not help but wonder if she was making an error in accepting Edwin's. And Lady Carsby's. And yet she had muddled matters so badly herself that last time with John that she did not dare to trust her own judgment.

"In any event," she said aloud, rising from her chair and beginning to pace about the room, "how am I to convince him that I love him and that he has mistaken my reasons for marriage? That I had nothing to do with Gilby's prank."

Calista paused. Honesty compelled her to add that even were John to forgive her she was not entirely ready to forgive *him*. It was therefore with a sigh that she sat down again at the writing desk and took up her pen. Briefly she wrote him that she had arrived in Bath and gave the address in Gay Street. Then Calista forced herself to describe gaily the sights she had seen that morning and comment that she looked forward to her first assembly that evening.

It was, she decided with a wry smile, precisely

the sort of letter to bring a frown to John's fore-
head and even, perhaps, cause him to gnash his
teeth. Quickly, before she could change her mind,
Calista sealed the letter and took it downstairs to
give into Mrs. Haverton's care. Mrs. Haverton
assured her that it would go out in that day's post.
Then Calista went back upstairs to look through
her dresses and decide which one to wear tonight.

It would not have been proper, of course, for
Calista to dance when she was still so newly in
mourning. But walking about the assembly rooms
she could see everyone who was in Bath and in
turn was soon spied by Lady Carsby. By then,
Edwin had already deserted her to dance with a
young girl he seemed to know. That, Calista
thought with a tiny frown, was a matter that
would bear watching.

Still, the moment Lady Carsby beckoned to her,
Calista moved to her side and dropped a curtsy.
She could not help being glad that she had worn
her dark blue silk dress, for she knew it became
her thought not, perhaps, as well as Lady Carsby's
pale blue satin and white lace dress became her.
As these thoughts ran through Calista's mind, her
brothers made their bows to Lady Carsby as well.

"Very prettily done," Lady Carsby said
approvingly. "But where is my great-nephew,
Edwin? And who are these young rapscallions?"

"Lady Carsby, may I present my brothers, Gilby
and Raynor?" Calista replied.

"How do you do?" Lady Carsby said graciously. "You've good manners at any rate. But where is Edwin?" she repeated.

Calista cast a worried look toward the dance floor. "I'm not quite certain," she confessed. "Almost as soon as we came in he mumbled something about seeing someone he knew and disappeared."

Lady Carsby's eyes were sharper than Calista's, however, and she said, also looking at the dancers, "There he is. With Henrietta Willoughby's girl. Edwin's mother won't like that. She and Henrietta never could abide one another, but it will serve her right if they make a match of it."

"A match of it?" Calista asked startled. "From one dance?"

Lady Carsby looked at Calista shrewdly. "You're not a fool, child. If Edwin sought out the chit the moment he arrived and, as I've no doubt he did, eagerly offered to accompany you here in the first place, then it seems most likely he had reason to know and to care that Miss Willoughby would be here. And that, my girl, argues an interest that goes well beyond sharing one dance together."

"You're right, of course," Calista said at once. Then, in a worried undertone she added, "I wonder what I should do about it?"

"Do about it?" Lady Carsby asked with lively astonishment. "Why should you do anything about it? After all, one could scarcely expect you to be Edwin's guardian. In any event, however much his mother might dislike the match, it would be a very advantageous one for the boy. No, you leave him be and think instead about your own future. And that of your brothers." Then, rising to her feet and closing her fan with a snap, she said, "Come along, the lot of you, and I'll introduce you to everyone I know."

Lady Carsby knew a great many people and she handled matters with rare tact. Before the evening was over, Calista and her brothers had been introduced to more people than they could remember. Lady Carsby had managed to convey, moreover, the information that Calista was Mrs. John Witton but had come to Bath to restore her spirits after the loss of her father. Just when the wedding had taken place was left quite vague and Lady Carsby forestalled all questions on the event by expressing astonishment that the person had not heard of it or of her great-nephew's attachment to the Standish girl.

"And that," she told Calista with satisfaction just before summoning a chair to take her home, "will take care of that. Just remember, child, to cultivate an air of modest confusion if asked about your attachment to John and refer all questions to him."

Unable to suppress an amused smile at this advice, Calista nevertheless pointed out, "Yes, but John is not here."

Lady Carsby chuckled. "He will be, my girl, he

will be. Within the fortnight, too, unless I much miss my guess. But you'd best decide by then just what you mean to tell him. Unless he's much changed since the last time I saw him, he's not the man to tolerate missish airs nor playacting. When you see him, speak your mind plainly and let him speak his."

"I'm afraid he may still be very angry with me," Calista said soberly.

"Let him be," Lady Carsby said roundly. "And don't be afraid of your own anger either. Unless I have you pegged very wrong, my girl, there's been some mistake on his part as well. You'll do best to resolve it now and not let it fester."

"I shall," Calista replied with a smile. She paused, then added, a trifle shakily, "Thank you for your help, and your advice, Lady Carsby."

"Nonsense!" Lady Carsby said sharply, though there was a distinct twinkle in her eyes. "I've taken a fancy to you, my girl, and that hasn't happened to me in some time. More to the point, I think you're just the wife for John and I'm glad to have a hand in making him happy. Even if he doesn't yet know that that's what will make him happy. And now enough of this gibber-jabbering. It's late and I want my bed. And if you'll take my advice you'll have your brothers call you a chair and go home as well."

"I shall," Calista promised.

Within the half hour she was back in Gay Street with Gilby, Raynor, and Edwin, listening to the

latter's praise of Miss Willoughby. With a chuckle
she left him talking to her brothers and sought her
own bed. For the first time since John had left for
London, Calista began to believe that her marriage
might yet be restored. And that was enough to
settle a foolish smile on her face as her maid
helped her prepare for bed.

17

IN THE DAYS that followed, when Calista was not taking a turn about the Parade Gardens or taking tea with Lady Carsby or with acquaintances introduced to her by her ladyship, or attending the Bath assemblies, she was to be found reading. There were any number of gentlemen who would have been pleased to introduce her to more lively amusements or arrange outings for her—she might not be a raving beauty, but there was a quiet charm about her and an undeniable air of mystery. But Calista declined all such invitations and was at home only to those gentlemen whose primary wish was to visit her brothers. However much Edwin and Lady Carsby might advise her to be seen enjoying herself, Calista could not bring herself to encourage the attentions of any gentleman.

Instead, Calista pronounced herself delighted to discover that there was an excellent lending library close upon the Pump Room and soon formed the habit of entering it each day to return a book and acquire a new one. Raynor was equally delighted, for it contained the works of a great many poets his father had disdained to have at Standish House.

Even Gilby, military mad as he was, was content to do so once he discovered that they carried the memoirs of a number of military greats as well. As for Edwin, he took the view that if he accompanied them there often enough, he was certain to encounter Miss Willoughby as she was a great reader of novels. And it could not be denied that within the week he began to encounter her there almost every day.

Following Lady Carsby's advice, Calista did not try to dissuade Edwin from talking with Miss Willoughby. She was sufficiently concerned, however, to write to John about the matter.

Had he been privileged to read it, Edwin would have taken great exception to the part of the letter that said, "Perhaps you will think it foolish of me, but I cannot help feeling concern that at such a young age your brother Edwin is paying such marked attention to one young lady. Miss Willoughby seems all that is amiable but I still cannot like it, particularly as Lady Carsby informs me your mother would dislike such a match excessively. How I wish there were someone here to advise me! I have asked Lady Carsby her opinion, but she seems to think it a great joke and tells me not to interfere. I do not ask you to come because I can well guess that you do not wish to see me. But Edwin is your brother and I wish you will write and tell me if there is anything I should do about the matter of Miss Willoughby."

Upon reading the letter in London, Witton paced about the room angrily, a habit he had developed increasingly with each letter from his wife in Bath. He had been on the point of setting out to Bath to bring Calista to book. Now he found himself wondering if she was using Edwin as an excuse to summon him to her side and he did not mean to be dictated to by anyone. All the old doubts about the openness of her character once more returned to assail him. Still, in the end, he gave the orders for his carriage to be brought around and loaded with the baggage for his trip to Bath. However much it might chafe him to ride in a closed carriage instead of his curricle, Witton meant to do so. For he equally meant to bring Calista either back to London with him or take her to Witton Manor himself as he ought to have done in the first place, and the carriage was a concession to her comfort.

Calista knew nothing of his plans, of course. Indeed, as the end of her first fortnight in Bath drew near, she found herself despairing at Lady Carsby's prediction that Witton would appear. Even her ladyship began to share Calista's concern. On the last day of that fortnight, she invited Calista to tea at her house in Great Pulteney Street. And she told her to come alone. "For," as she told Calista bluntly when she arrived, "I mean to speak frankly about my great-nephew and that I cannot do with a bunch of young men about. I'll not admit the folly of my advice, if folly it was, to them."

When Calista was seated in the drawing room and the tea poured, Lady Carsby looked at her sharply and said, "I spoke of my folly, child, and now let us talk of yours! Why haven't you put your time in Bath to better use? I've done my best, introducing you to all my acquaintances, including a number of most eligible men. And you've wasted it all, not once accepting any invitations to go for a drive with a gentleman, or walk about the gardens with anyone except your brothers, and while I do not suggest you should have danced, there are ways to keep a gentleman at your side talking at an assembly, my dear. How is my nephew to be made jealous if you won't make the least push to seem interested in anyone else?"

Calista set her teacup down gently and forced herself to speak frankly as she said, "I meant to, Lady Carsby, but I soon found I could not, that indeed I had no wish to do so."

"What has that to say to the matter?" Lady Carsby asked tartly. "I did not ask you to marry the fellows, merely accept their company often enough that someone would tell your fool of a husband and bring him posthaste to Bath."

"But that's just it," Calista went on, with a troubled frown, "that's just what I did not want to do. There has been enough trouble, enough misunderstanding between us as it is, I could not add to the score."

"Well," Lady Carsby said grudgingly, "there is something in what you say. But where the devil is my great-nephew? I was certain John would be here by now."

Calista hesitated then said, "I have written him, Lady Carsby, to tell him of Edwin's interest in Miss Willoughby."

"You've what?" she demanded incredulously.

Calista met her ladyship's eyes calmly. "I know you favor the match," she said coolly, "and it is not to stop it that I wrote John. But because I think Edwin may be contemplating some folly."

"Folly?" Lady Carsby frowned as she repeated the word. "What the devil do you mean, child?"

It was Calista's turn to frown. She stood and took a turn about the room, before she answered. "I am not entirely sure," she said. "But Edwin has more than once told me that he knows his mother will never approve of Miss Willoughby and that for once in his life he means not to be bound by her words. That he will do whatever he finds necessary. And I own that I find it strange that such a high-spirited boy has been bound by them for as long as this."

Lady Carsby shot her young guest a sharp look before she said, "I take it then you've not spent long in Mrs. Witton's company or you would know how overbearing she can be. You also cannot know that the boy was quite ill in his younger days and it became natural for my niece to cosset him and keep him close about her skirts. And once my niece's husband died there was no hope anyone would stand up for the boy. John was too eager to escape her grasp himself. And Octavia would never have consented to place him in John's care willingly, whatever the will might have said about guardianship!''

Lady Carsby paused, then added a bit more quietly, ''I own it disturbs me to hear Edwin is speaking this way. It's true I'd approve a match between him and Miss Willoughby, but one done right. Nothing havey-cavey or so foolish as a flight to Gretna Green or some such nonsense. I'll tell you what, my girl, when you go back to Gay Street, send the boy to me. I'll talk to him. It may be that if he knows how strongly I'll back him against Octavia, he'll give over this nonsense.''

''I shall do so, and I thank you, Lady Carsby,'' Calista said warmly.

They talked for some time longer and then Calista took her leave.

Back in the private parlor in Gay Street Calista had just set down her bonnet when Mrs. Haverton knocked timidly on the door of the room. ''Pray come in,'' Calista said kindly, for she had taken a liking to the woman.

''Oh, I must not,'' Mrs. Haverton said, a trifle tremulously. ''I've some things to do, but one of the young gentlemen, Master Edwin, left a note for you. And . . . and there was another gentleman who called. He . . . he claimed to be your husband, ma'am."

"John?" Calista said faintly, the color draining from her face. "John was here?"

"Yes, ma'am. John Witton, he said his name was. I said he was welcome to wait, but he said that as none of you but Master Edwin were home he would go looking for you."

"Edwin was here then?" Calista asked, beginning to hope that perhaps he had managed to tell her husband the truth.

These hopes were dashed, however, as Mrs. Haverton said, "Yes, and what a row there was between the pair of them. That's when Mr. Witton went out and Master Edwin shortly after him. And gave me the note to give you."

"Thank you," Calista said, turning away so that Mrs. Haverton might not see the tears gathering in her eyes.

Mrs. Haverton left the room, closing the door gently behind her. Calista opened the note from Edwin and with gathering dismay read the message he had left for her.

Dear Cal,

You're going to be very angry with me, I know, but please believe I haven't any other choice. I've run away. With Miss Willoughby if she'll go with me. Her mother don't like the match any better than mine and we've made up our

minds that it's the North Road for us.
Thank you for your kindness, and say
goodbye to your brothers for me. You're
a capital family.

Affectionately yours,
Edwin Witton

Appalled, Calista did not stop to change her
dress but immediately placed the bonnet back on
her head and went out to go around to the
Willoughby residence. There she was met with the
information that Miss Willoughby had gone out
for a walk in the gardens with her maid some time
before and no one knew when she would be back.

Calista did not waste time asking further questions but headed for the posting house that served
the northernmost route out of Bath. If Edwin was
bent on leaving Bath with Miss Willoughby, that
was where she would find word of him and, with
luck, stop him before the pair even set out. Which
she hoped to do, for if Miss Willoughby had gone
out early enough, Edwin might not yet have
spoken with her. But knowing the boy, Calista
thought grimly to herself, he would not hesitate to
make the arrangements anyway.

At the posting house she discovered the
situation to be worse than she had thought. The
ostler had news of a pair, matching their descrip-
tion, leaving the inn not half an hour earlier.

Calista found herself in a quandary. That it was
most improper for her to hire a carriage and go

after the pair alone she could not doubt. But Mrs. Haverton had not known where Gilby and Raynor had gone, nor did Calista wish to waste time searching for them when it might cost her any chance she had of catching up with the eloping pair. Telling herself that she was, after all, a married woman and not some green girl, Calista resolutely ordered another carriage readied and the horses put to. Within the hour she was on the road after Edwin and Miss Willoughby.

Behind her, in the house in Gay Street, John Witton was once more pacing the room that served as a private parlor for Mrs. Haverton's lodgers. That lady was twisting her hands together nervously as she answered his irate questions. "But I tell you, I don't know where Mrs. Witton has gone!"

"No, of course not," he answered sardonically. "You can only tell me that she heard the news of my arrival and left at once. To escape seeing me, no doubt."

"Oh, sir, I'm certain it wasn't that way," Mrs. Haverton protested.

"No?" Witton demanded ruthlessly. "Next I suppose you will tell me she was all delight at the news of my arrival."

"Well, no," Mrs. Haverton admitted reluctantly.

"And did she tell you nothing?" Witton persisted.

Mrs. Haverton shook her head. And with a sigh of exasperation, Witton once more went downstairs, meaning to go out and look for his wife. He paused only to ask a little boy hanging about outside if he had seen the lady who had been staying upstairs.

"Yes sir, she went out a short time ago," the lad replied at once. "I heard her tell the hackney driver she wished to go to a Miss Willoughby's house on Somerset Place."

"Hmmm, come to that, I ought to pay a visit there, myself," Witton said to himself thoughtfully.

Aloud, he thanked the boy and gave him a shilling. Then Witton summoned a hackney as well, his own carriage having been sent round to the stables already.

The Willoughbys were not at home nor was Calista there, but a street sweeper had overheard her direct the coachman to the inn that served the North Road. Witton gave the same instructions to his hackney driver. If Calista were bent on fleeing him, out of Bath if need be, as he began to fear, he would follow. Yes, and rent the fastest rig he could in order to catch her. It was fortunate that his traveling coach was safely stabled, Witton began to think. He had no wish for his servants to hear of this latest turn of events. Nor was his cumbersome coach the best thing to use if one wished to travel quickly. And Witton meant to travel very quickly indeed.

18

Luck was with Calista and she caught up with the pair when they paused for supper at a posting house near Nailsworth. It was apparent as she stepped into the Swan Inn that both Edwin and Miss Willoughby were tired and engaged in an argument. Although the proprietor had allotted them the coffee room, he was not in the least reluctant to show Calista into that parlor as soon as she informed the fellow that she was Edwin's sister-in-law.

Mopping his brow he told her, "I much mislike the look of things, ma'am, and it's grateful I am that you're here. I don't hold with such goings-on and the pair of them look as though they need someone to take them in hand."

"Don't worry, I shall," Calista said coolly.

Without knocking she entered the small parlor and immediately closed the door behind her. In a glance she took in the plates of cold food that had been set before the pair and which no doubt accounted in part for Miss Willoughby's sulky expression. Edwin stood by the window, frozen for a moment with the shock of seeing Calista. He was, however, the first to speak. "Cal! What are you doing here? Never mind that, explain to Jennifer that one cannot always command a hot meal as one wishes."

Calmly stripping off her gloves and removing her bonnet, Calista addressed Miss Willoughby. "That is quite true, you know," she said. "Though I will allow that it can be most vexing when one is tired and hungry and that I would have expected better of the place than cold mutton. Still, that is one of the hazards one must expect if one chooses to elope. One cannot afford, after all, to stop at the best inns where one might be recognized by someone."

"I told you so," Edwin said triumphantly. Then, suspiciously, he turned to Calista and asked, "Why did you come? Not to stop us, I hope, for you can't."

Calista had been prepared for the question. Indeed, she had spent much of her journey thinking of what she would say to Edwin. "I came to discover, if I could, why you are taking such a step."

"We had no other choice, Mrs. Witton," Miss Willoughby said softly.

"But why not?" Calista asked reasonably. "To be sure, I have understood that Mrs. Witton would not like the match, but I do not see how she could have forbidden it. Not when John is your guardian and you have not even asked him what he thinks.

Why are you so certain he will oppose it? Particularly as the Willoughbys countenance the match. You are both of you young enough that the time it would take to bring John around surely can not seem so very formidable. Even Lady Carsby stands your champion."

"But my parents don't countenance the match," Jennifer protested.

Startled, Calista turned her fine eyes on the girl. "Surely you are mistaken, Miss Willoughby! In Bath there was no hint of your parents' disapproval. Why I have heard your mother invite Edwin to come to call. Nor do I recollect her ever forbidding you to go out walking with him. Perhaps you misunderstood and they meant they wished you to wait awhile."

Edwin shook his head. "I wish it were as simple as that," he said bitterly. "You have heard Aunt Grace speak of my mother's dislike for Mrs. Willoughby, well it seems the feeling is mutual."

He paused and Jennifer took up the tale. "It seems my Mama wanted Edwin to ... to fall in love with me so that she could snub his pretensions when he went to speak to my father. And that is just what he did. Papa said he would never countenance a match between our two families."

"And then John arrived in Bath today and threatened to drag me off home again while Jennifer's parents mean to take her to travel on the continent. Surely you must see there was no time to be wasted," Edwin pleaded eloquently.

"What I see is that the pair of you have taken a step that bids fair to ruin both of you," Calista said tartly. "Could you not have stopped to ask my advice?"

"There wasn't time, I tell you," Edwin replied. "Besides, what could you have proposed?"

That was a poser. In the post chaise Calista had made up her mind to invite Miss Willoughby to come and stay with her, back at the Standish household, or, if she and John managed to patch things up between them, wherever he wished to live. But if her parents were indeed so opposed to the Witton family, they would surely not agree to such a scheme. "I am not entirely sure," she confessed. "But I do know that this is not a solution."

"What do you mean to do?" Jennifer asked softly.

Calista smiled at her kindly. "For the moment, stay here with you while you try to eat and while I have some food myself. Then we may discuss it. At the very least, my presence will in some small measure ease your situation. We might even be able to persuade your parents to give out that you both came with me back to my parents' home in the country. Mr. and Mrs. Willoughby will not like it, but I cannot believe they would prefer to have the world know you meant to elope."

"Is that what you truly wish to do?" Jennifer asked shyly. "Edwin has told me that your husband is in Bath."

"Of course not," Calista replied tranquilly. "What I should prefer is to return to Bath tonight. Your parents may then give out that we meant to go to my family home but that when word reached me that my husband was in Bath, we returned post haste. Or, if they will not agree to that, you shall return with me and we shall say that we went for a drive together and my carriage broke down."

"Then we shall return to Bath with you, Mrs. Witton," Jennifer said quietly, "for I do believe you truly mean to stand our friend."

"But what about Gretna Green?" Edwin protested.

Calista looked at her brother-in-law coolly. "What of it?" she asked. "Do you mean to say that you prefer to start your marriage under a cloud rather than make a push to wed Miss Willoughby properly?"

Edwin did not at once answer but rather looked at her mutinously. It was left to Miss Willoughby to say timidly, "It is so very far to Scotland, Edwin, and you know how the carriage was already giving me the headache. And the food has not been so very good and you were telling me yourself we should find ourselves tight on funds before we were through. And for some time after the wedding."

"Oh, very well," Edwin said at last. "It's back to Bath, I suppose. But mind, I don't mean to let your parents separate us again."

"If we are to return to Bath tonight," Miss

Willoughby said in her soft voice, "then I should like to go upstairs and tidy up first."

"Of course," Calista told her warmly.

When she was gone Edwin turned to his sister-in-law. "I'm afraid I've caused you a great deal of trouble," he said.

"So you have," Calista agreed frankly. "But what is done is done. I blame myself for not speaking with you sooner."

"I ought to have confided in you," Edwin admitted. "But I haven't the habit of doing so with anyone, you see."

As he spoke there was a commotion in the passageway outside the coffee room and, a moment later, the door was flung open. To the surprise of Calista and Edwin, John Witton stood in the doorway, blinking with an astonishment that matched their own. "Good God!" he managed at last. "Edwin! I had not thought it possible. Have you no sense of decency?"

Edwin colored to the roots of his hair but to his credit did not stumble as he replied stoutly, "I mean to marry her as soon as I am able to do so, even though Cal has convinced me that Gretna Green is not the answer after all."

As the color drained from *his* face, John turned to Calista. His voice lost nothing of its fury, however, as he said, "Did you indeed, madam? How very wise of you. I suppose it did not occur to my brother all the difficulties there might be. Even in Scotland."

"No, it did not," Calista agreed evenly, her own face very pale. "His education, in that respect, is sadly lacking. I wonder you never took him in hand and saw to the matter."

"I?" Witton laughed sharply. "You are mistaken, madam. I could not have foreseen such a situation as this," he flung at her.

White with rage Calista replied, "I daresay not, since you have taken so little interest in Edwin. But surely you must have realized that any young man ought to know about elopements, and surely you know something about those."

"Oh, indeed," Witton agreed, ruthlessly cutting her short, "I have encountered elopements before. But never when another man's wife was involved."

"Another man's wife?" Edwin demanded incredulously. "What the devil are you talking about?"

Calista, however, was not so slow in understanding. After staring at Witton for a moment with a somewhat dazed expression, she lowered her eyes and, in an unsteady voice, asked, "John, just what did you think was happening when you came after me?"

"I thought that hearing I was in Bath, you had run away from me," Witton replied frankly. "I suppose Edwin told you I was in a devil of a mood when I arrived. But that was because I believed the farrago of nonsense you wrote me about him and Miss Willoughby. I had not realized, until he spoke of Gretna Green just now, how matters really stood between you. I suppose that all this nonsense about Miss Willoughby was meant to serve as a smokescreen of sorts so that no one would realize how close you and he had become?"

Edwin would have spoken, but Calista waved him to be silent. She rose to her feet and walked over to the fireplace. Staring down into it she said, over her shoulder, "No, that part was true. Edwin is much attached to Miss Willoughby and she to him. You'd best make up your mind to help them or they may yet run off to Gretna Green."

She paused and turned to face him now. Her eyes met his steadily as she said, in a voice devoid of emotion, "Miss Willoughby is here, you know. Upstairs, tidying herself up before the journey back to Bath. I ought, of course, to have left you a note, telling you what I was about. But I wasn't thinking very clearly just then. I knew you and Edwin had quarreled and I hoped, in any event, to catch the pair before they left Bath. And when I found I could not, I did not think to send around a message to Gay Street before setting out. My only thought was to catch up with them as soon as possible."

As Calista spoke, John was crossing the room to her side. Before she had done talking his hands were on her shoulders, shaking her. "Are you telling me the truth?" he demanded ruthlessly.

From behind them Edwin spoke. "Of course she is. But if she had run away from you, John, it would have been your own fault," he said sharply.

"So far as I can see, you haven't treated Cal very well at all. It would have served you right if someone had decided to take her to Gretna Green."

Before John could answer, the door to the parlor opened once more and Miss Willoughby stepped in, carefully closing the door behind her. "Who are you?" Witton demanded, a snap in his voice.

"Miss Willoughby," Calista replied dryly.

"Jenny?" John asked, startled. "I have not seen you in some time."

"And I am no longer a little girl," she finished for him. "You are angry at Edwin and myself and I cannot wonder at it, but pray lower your voice, it can be heard throughout the inn."

"Yes, of course," he said at once. "But we must be thinking of getting you back to Bath. And what we shall tell your parents. Did you leave a note?"

Jennifer shook her head. "There was no time," she said quietly. "Edwin found me walking in the park and persuaded me that we must come straightaway. I did not even tell my maid where I was going." She colored, then said resolutely, "I told her that Mrs. Witton had asked for me and that Edwin was escorting me to her and that she would see me home later."

In spite of herself, Calista laughed. "I see nothing humorous in the situation," John told her curtly.

Calista shook her head. "No, of course not," she

said, "but I am impressed with Miss Willoughby's foresight."

"And I am appalled at her imagination," John retorted ruthlessly. "She has dragged you into this situation by her thoughtlessness. What if you had not gone after the pair and the Willoughbys came to call upon you and demanded that you produce their daughter."

At once Jennifer looked stricken. To Calista she said, "I am sorry. I had not thought it might lead to unpleasantness for you. It is just that that was the only excuse I could think of quickly, and I did need to get rid of my maid."

"Of course you did," Calista replied soothingly. "And really, this makes matters quite simple. We shall say that I asked you to go for a drive with me and our carriage sustained an accident, which is why we are returning so very late. That tale will do for the servants and anyone else who asks."

"But I thought we were to say that I was on my way to stay with your family," Miss Willoughby protested.

Calista shook her head. "I must have been very tired when I said so. It will not do, you see, for you brought no baggage with you. No one will believe you came away, with your parents' consent, without baggage. I think it must be the story that we went for a drive together, instead."

"Yes," Witton agreed thoughtfully, "but the Willoughbys must be told the truth. Otherwise we shall find ourselves in just such a mess again shortly. Mind, I am not saying I countenance the match, but neither do I underestimate, any longer, the strength of their attachment."

Calista told him calmly, ". . . I shall speak to them when I return, Miss Willoughby."

"I shall be there as well," Witton said curtly.

Calista regarded him with raised eyebrows. "If you and Edwin—for I don't see how you could stop him from accompanying you—should arrive with us, that will fan the gossip."

"Won't it be rather late?" Jennifer put in timidly. "My parents will not be at their best just then."

Witton moved to where Miss Willoughby stood and took her hand in his. "You are right," he told her. "My wife shall simply see you home and together we shall call upon your parents in the morning. We will all be better for a good night's sleep."

Calista raised her eyebrows at this piece of high-handedness but did not protest. "Hadn't we best be going?" was all she said.

A few minutes sufficed to take care of Edwin's carriage and ensure that the driver would return it empty to Bath, for he meant to ride with his brother. As they walked to her carriage, Calista could not help remarking to Witton, "Gilby and Raynor must be very worried by now."

"You ought to have thought of that beforehand," John said curtly.

"No doubt I should have if I had not had more

urgent matters on my mind," Calista retorted tartly.

He did not answer. Afraid to look at the man who was her husband but who seemed such a stranger at the moment, Calista allowed him to hand her into the carriage. Edwin had already helped Miss Willoughby inside and as soon as the door had been closed, they were on their way back to Bath.

19

CALISTA WAS EXTREMELY weary by the time she reached the house in Gay Street. The Willoughbys had been grateful to have their daughter restored to them but suspicious of the part Calista had played, and she had been glad to escape their questions. She had, however, promised to call in the morning and explain everything.

When she returned to Gay Street and entered the private parlor, she found Gilby and Raynor waiting up for her. "Where the devil have you been?" Gilby demanded.

"Do you know Witton is in town?" Raynor added.

"And have you any idea what's happened to Edwin?" Gilby persisted. "No one's seen him all day."

Silently Calista set her bonnet down on the table and took her time in answering her brothers. At last she said quietly, "I went for a drive and have just returned. As for Edwin, he will be back shortly, I think, with John."

"Yes, but where were you?" Raynor demanded.

"I shan't tell you, for it is none of your affair," Calista replied remorselessly.

It would be unreasonable to suppose that these answers satisfied the two Standish boys. But as Calista refused to tell them anything more, they were forced at last to retreat to their own room to talk over matters between themselves. "And you should get some sleep," was Gilby's parting shot to her.

Calista gave him a wan smile. "I cannot," she said with a shake of her head. "I expect John to arrive directly and will wait up for him."

As she spoke there was the sound of an outer door opening and shutting and footsteps on the stairs. Gilby shot Calista a sharp look. "Are you certain you don't want us to stay?" he asked. "It's our tale, you know, that caused the trouble in the first place."

Again Calista shook her head. "No, this is a matter that must be settled between ourselves, whatever the circumstances that began it."

So, reluctantly, Gilby and Raynor took themselves off to bed. A moment later the door to the parlor opened and unconsciously Calista gripped the arms of the chair she sat in tightly.

John Witton was tired also. He had done a great deal of traveling that day and his temper was not of the best. But his sharp eyes did not miss the pallor of Calista's face nor the hint of fear in her eyes, and his expression softened. He did not enter the room all the way but said gently, "Go to bed,

Calista. We shall sort out everything in the morning."

"And . . . and you?" she asked, her voice strained.

Now Witton came into the room as Calista rose to her feet. Gently he took her hands in his and kissed the top of her head. "I think it best, my dear, that we sort things out between us first. I shall share Edwin's room tonight."

Not trusting herself to speak, Calista nodded and left to go to her own room. But her thoughts and tears kept sleep at bay for some time.

The next morning Calista dressed as she had the first day she met John, in the mauve jaconet muslin with the black trim. He seemed not to notice. After a hasty, strained breakfast, she and John and Edwin presented themselves at the Willoughby household. It was evident that Jennifer had already put her parents in possession of the facts, for as soon as the footman had gone and the door to the drawing room been closed, Mr. Willoughby spoke frankly.

"I understand, Mrs. Witton, that I have you to thank for my daughter's return last night. And your quick wits for a tale to tell the servants to cover the truth."

"Believe me when I say your daughter and Edwin had already come to realize something of their folly when I found them," Calista answered earnestly.

"Folly indeed!" Mrs. Willoughby sniffed loudly.

"As to that," John said gravely, "I believe there to have been great provocation that led to their folly."

"Provocation?" Mr. Willoughby demanded, taken aback. "How dare you say so?"

It was John's turn to be surprised. "Am I mistaken, then, in thinking that you oppose a match between my brother and your daughter?"

"We most certainly do oppose such a match," Mrs. Willoughby said haughtily. "As does your mother, I am sure."

"Then you ought to have been honest enough to say so," Calista told Mrs. Willoughby quietly. "Instead, you encouraged Edwin to dangle after your daughter. That was foolish beyond permission."

"I only meant to teach him a lesson," Mrs. Willoughby protested.

"Because of your feud with my mother, I suppose," Witton said grimly. "But you have hurt your daughter as well."

Mrs. Willoughby's eyes took on a distinctly martial gleam. Mr. Willoughby, however, had had enough. Testily he said, "Yes, yes, everyone is at fault. The question now is what to do about it. Your story satisfied the servants and no one else knows she was gone. And we shall take Jenny to the Continent. That will put an end to this nonsense."

Standing beside him, Calista could hear Witton sigh before he addressed Mr. Willoughby.

"However much both families may dislike it, my brother and your daughter have developed a *tendre* for one another," he said curtly. "And I do not rate their resolution so lightly as you seem to do. Nor can I continue to be so deaf to their feelings when they have shown us the attachment runs so deep."

"Indeed?" Mrs. Willoughby demanded angrily. "What are you suggesting that we do?"

A ghost of a smile played about Witton's lips as he replied, "May I venture to guess, ma'am, that your daughter has not yet had a London Season? I know very well that Edwin has not paid a visit there."

"Jennifer was to have made her comeout next spring, after she acquired a bit of polish here in Bath." Mrs. Willoughby admitted grudgingly. "But what is that to the point?"

"Just this: I propose that we haul off the both of them to London and let them taste the social life there. Let them look about and see what is to be seen and if, after a year, they are of the same mind, then agree to let them marry," Witton said quietly.

That produced an uproar. Between the elder Willoughbys vowing never to consent to the match so easily and Jennifer and Edwin protesting that a year was far too long, it was almost impossible to hear oneself speak. In the end, however, all were brought to agree, however grudgingly, to the scheme. "Though mind, young man, I don't like it and neither will your mother," Henrietta Willoughby warned Witton.

"My mother," he replied coolly, "will have nothing to say to the matter."

"Oh, yes she will," Mr. Willoughby countered gloomily. "The question is, can you and your brother stand up to her."

Briefly, Witton smiled a wintery smile. "I think so."

Willoughby nodded. Then, sighing heavily, he went on, "Well, that's taken care of. And I suppose that personal feelings and their age aside, there is little to say against the match. I assume the boy has expectations, even if he is a younger son?"

"He does," Witton confirmed dryly.

"Well then," Willoughby said, "we will postpone our plans for the Continent. Instead, we shall try your scheme and remove to London to give Jenny a taste of the *ton*. When do you go there, sir?"

"And me, you mean," Edwin added impudently.

John directed a quelling look at his brother, then addressed Mr. Willoughby, taking care to avoid looking in Calista's direction. "My wife and her brothers and my brother and I are returning shortly to her family home. After a brief stay there, we mean to go directly to London. Unless my wife decides that she wishes to visit my family home. Our plans are not yet altogether decided, but even so within a month we should be in London."

"I see," Willoughby replied. "Then we shall no doubt be seeing you. Mrs. Witton, I must thank you once again for helping my daughter out of the pickle these young people got themselves into."

Calista brushed aside the thanks and soon she and John and Edwin took their leave. The Willoughbys made no attempt to keep them.

Back at the house in Gay Street, Witton sent Calista upstairs saying that he wished to speak with Edwin and would be up directly. When she opened the parlor door, Calista found herself facing a young woman dressed in a walking dress of pale pink silk with white flounces. She was standing by the window and regarded Calista with the greatest interest.

"May I help you?" Calista asked doubtfully.

The woman came forward and held out her hand in a friendly way. "Actually," she said kindly, "I am hoping that I may be able to help you. I am Eleanor Leverton."

"How do you do," Calista replied, trying to conceal her astonishment.

"I hope you do not mind," Eleanor went on calmly, "but I prevailed upon your brothers to go out so that we might have a comfortable coze together. I wanted to see the girl John had married. And to warn you that he is coming to Bath."

Coloring faintly, Calista turned away and said,

the constraint evident in her voice, "Yes, I know. He is already here."

"And he has made a sad botch of things," Eleanor said bluntly, "has he not?"

"Perhaps it is I who have made a sad botch of things," Calista countered.

"Perhaps," Eleanor agreed, "but will you not sit down and talk with me? I have a great fondness for John and, I think, for you."

Startled, Calista replied, "But you do not know me."

"Ah, but I have heard a great deal about you," Eleanor countered with laughing eyes, "both from John and from my husband. And I think you are just the girl for him. I thought so in London, from what they said, and now that I see you, I am more certain of it than ever. You have the same look about you that he does. And that is why I came: to see if you and I might put our heads together and patch things up between you two. That is, if you do love him," she concluded, a trifle anxiously.

"I do," Calista replied simply.

"Then it only wants a little resolution," Eleanor said triumphantly, "and the matter is settled."

"Is it?" A voice from the doorway startled them both. Then, before they could reply, Witton added, "And where, by the by, is Freddy?"

At once Eleanor was on her feet and crossing the room to where he stood. "At the hotel, with the baby. I told him I wished to see your bride for myself, by myself. We wanted to warn her you were coming. Infamous of you to have driven all the way in under twenty-four hours, for I collect that is what you must have done. When did you arrive?"

"Yesterday," he replied curtly. "And what is this nonsense about matters only requiring a little resolution?" he added, more kindly.

"Well, of course they do, John," she told him with a little pout. "How you can have been so foolish as to believe anything ill of Calista is beyond me! Now that I have met her I cannot credit any aspersions on her character. She hasn't the look of—of a Maria."

"You are very kind," Calista told Eleanor, coloring again, "but I beg you will not say so. It—it is not so simple as it seems."

"Why not?" Eleanor demanded. When neither Witton nor Calista answered her, she retreated to a corner chair, sat down, and said, with a wave of her hand, "Don't regard me! Pretend I am not even here."

"You are not going to be," Witton told her bluntly.

"Yes, but I wish to stay and see that you do not browbeat poor Calista," Eleanor told him.

Witton knew her well enough not to waste any further breath arguing. Instead, he pointed to the door. Meekly Eleanor went out, pouting. Then he turned to Calista and said, "How do you go on here in Bath?"

"What do you mean?" Calista parried. "There

are assemblies and teas, and Lady Carsby has been kind enough to introduce me to a number of her acquaintances.''

Witton drew in his breath sharply. "In short, you have been enjoying yourself excessively?" he asked.

Repressing a strong desire to break into tears, Calista blinked rapidly as she said, "Why not? Did you think that just because I am of a scholarly turn of mind I cannot enjoy other things as well? I told you once that I wanted to go to London parties and balls and such. Did you not believe me?"

"Edwin spoke of other gentlemen. Have there been any?" he asked evenly.

Calista met his eyes squarely as she replied, anger evident in her voice, "If you have spoken with anyone here you know very well there have not been.''

He did not at once answer and after a moment she half turned away as she said, in so low a voice that he had to strain to hear, "I have not just been wasting my days in frivolity, if that is what you fear. There have been a great many letters to answer; my father had a great many correspondents who must be written to."

"Surely that is your mother's responsibility?" Witton suggested coolly.

In spite of herself, Calista laughed at the notion and her eyes were dancing as she looked at him and said, "Oh, John, I can quite see Mama trying to explain to Sir John Soane Papa's latest notions on architecture or Egyptian hieroglyphics. Or his researches in astronomy to Sir William Herschel. Or his suggestions to Sir David Brewster on the matter of kaleidoscopes, can't you?''

Witton grinned appreciatively at the thought. Then his face turned grave again as he went on, ''I can see that your acquaintances in London will quite outshine mine. We shall be known for giving the oddest and most famous of parties.''

''Shall we?'' Calista asked quizzically, tilting her head to one side. ''I thought you meant to send me to Witton Manor, to rusticate on my own. Isn't that why you came? To make me go there?''

Once more Witton hesitated. Then he said, ''I have spoken with Gilby and Raynor. And with Edwin,'' he added as an afterthought.

''Have—have you?'' Calista asked, avoiding his gaze.

''Yes. And I am as angry as ever at Gilby,'' Witton said implacably. ''I mean to purchase colors for him as soon as possible, whatever your mother may think of such a thing. He needs the discipline of the military.''

Calista's eyes flew up to meet his. ''I know it was an infamous thing for Gilby to do,'' she said, ''but I swear I knew nothing about it.''

Witton moved to stand beside his wife. Taking her hands in his he said, ''Do you know, when I discovered that you were gone yesterday, that you had fled from me, I also discovered that I no longer cared whether you knew or not. I only knew that I wanted you back. Then, today, when Gilby told me the whole, I knew I had been grossly unfair to you. We have a great deal to sort out, it seems. If you still wish to do so."

Calista looked up at him as she said frankly, "I had the oddest notion that perhaps you had decided we shouldn't suit."

"Why should we not?" Witton asked quietly.

Calista looked away. "Oh, a thousand reasons," she said in a voice filled with constraint. "You are a—a top of the trees fellow, bang up to the nines with town bronze. And I am something of a drab sparrow."

"Never that!" Witton countered, crushing Calista to him and kissing her ruthlessly.

"I—I won't go to Witton Manor," she said, when he let her loose a few minutes later. "Not without you."

There was a hint of laughter in his eyes as he answered her. "You shan't have to. I mean to keep you by my side, whether in London or in the country. Wherever you wish to be." He paused, then said gently, "I know that I meant to send you to Witton Manor to punish you, but it is a perfectly good country house, you know. It isn't as old as yours, or filled with so much history, but my father built it to be quite comfortable. There is a delightful library, far larger than your father's, light and airy with doors that open into the gardens. And there is a lake and any number of follies and conceits. Even a little waterfall. You could have as large a laboratory as you wished and I promise I shouldn't complain no matter how many sailors arrived to bring you plants and things from far away. You could experiment and study as much as you wished, with my absolute blessing."

Calista laughed and then said, in an innocent voice, "Do you mean you shan't even complain if I contrive to blow things up?"

"Not so long as you do not blow yourself up as well," he growled down at her.

Calista smiled, but shook her head sadly and turned away. "You—you cannot mean it," she said with some constraint.

This time Witton placed his hands on her shoulders as he said gently, "Why not, dear one?" She shivered under his touch but he did not let go. "Why not, dear one?" he repeated, this time in a more determined tone.

Calista turned to look up at him. Her eyes were troubled as she said, "You know about Gilby. I cannot believe you wish to be married to someone you were forced into wedding. Someone you believe married you to gain her money."

A wry smile settled itself on Witton's face as he said, "My foolish Calista, how can you say I was forced to marry you? You know you tried to dissuade me yourself."

"You said before—" Calista began, with a catch in her throat.

"I have said a great deal of nonsense," Witton replied soberly. "Can you forgive me for that?" He waited until she nodded before he went on, anxiously, "Will you come and be my wife?"

Again she nodded and was swept up once more into his crushing embrace. At that moment, Eleanor poked her head in the door and gave a crow of triumph. "I knew it!" she said. "I knew you were suited and that if I lent a hand we should patch things up in a trice! How pleased Freddy will be to hear the news."

Witton lifted his lips from Calista's long enough to look at his friend's wife and tell her, bluntly, "Then I wish you will go away and tell him. At once!"